Three Guys Talking 3: The Romantic Tragedy

Three Guys Talking 3: The Romantic Tragedy

Book 3

Adeyinka O. Laiyemo, MD, MPH

DEDICATION

This novel is dedicated to those who go above and beyond the call of duty to help others especially during this COVID 19 pandemic.

ACKNOWLEDGMENTS

To the glory of the Almighty, I say a heartfelt thank you to all of you from A to Z for your assistance, encouragement, and support. Thank you for taking the tough and emotional social journey with the three poor guys.

FROM THE AUTHOR

Thank you for your interest in this third and concluding episode of the trilogy *Three Guys Talking,* a romantic seriocomic chronicle of the love lives of Adam Gray, Kamal Brown, and Ray Marshall from their points of view.

In the end, the decision was made for Adam. Adam got married. Nora got married. Aneida got married. Richard got married. Are they happy in their marriages? Only time will tell.

Bonita and Kamal sourced the money and went for in-Vitro Fertilization. It is uncertain that it will result in successful delivery of a baby. Meanwhile, Kandie alleged immigration violation and gave information to the Department of Homeland and Sea Security, Immigration and Customs Enforcement section in an attempt to have Bonita and her family deported from the United States. In the end, Kamal made his decision and decided for himself what struggle is worth struggling for.

Ray got a part-time job to teach *Law and Ethics* in a community college for the additional income his family needs but soon found out that challenges are like weeds in a lawn, they breed and invite other weeds. Meanwhile, Desiree wanted to prove her friend wrong by going back to school and joining the workforce, but her family responsibilities are in the way. Should she get a live-in nanny to help her with all her responsibilities? In the end, Ray had to make his decision too.

Contents

Prologue

(In my mind: from Ray to Desiree)
<u>**Nothing compares to my love for you**</u>

I am sure you don't know that
My love for you is so high
If it is a mountain
Mount Everest will be like a molehill

I don't think you know that
My love for you is so large
If it is a liquid
The Pacific Ocean will be like a cup of water

I think you don't know that
My love for you is so hot
If it is a particle
A supernova explosion will be like a blast of winter

I feel you don't know that
My love for you is so great
If it is a structure
The Great Wall of China will be like a brick

I know you don't know that
My love for you is so heavy
If it is matter
The black hole will be like featherweight

I don't know if you know that
My love for you is so sweet
If it is a substance
Honey will taste like bile

I don't think you know that
My love for you is so soft and tender
If it is touchable
Jelly fish will feel like sandpaper

I don't think you know that
My love for you is so sparkling
If it could be seen
Polished diamond will look like tar

I don't think you know that
My love for you is so smoot
If it is a fabric
Velvet will feel like burlap

The message from Ray to Desiree: "My love for you is comparable to none. This is the truth. **Please change for the better**."

(In my mind: from Kamal to Bonita)
Taking comfort in you
You are like an ice cream cone
For a child on a summer afternoon
Haaaa! So inviting

You are like a glass of milk
For a man who is eating Oreo cookies
Haaaa! So satisfying

You are like a wonderful balm
For a man's bruised ego
Haaaa! So soothing

You are like an umbrella
For a man on a very hot day
Haaaa! So shielding

You are like a winter coat of fur
For a man whose car broke down in a blizzard
Haaaa! So protecting

You are like a bulletproof vest
For a cop responding to a bank robbery
Haaaa! So defending

You are like a perfect massage
For a tight muscle after a hard day's work
Haaaa! So relaxing

You are like a bottle of cold water
For a thirsty man in the desert
Haaaa! So fulfilling

The message from Kamal to Bonita: "Thank you for being alluring, exciting, and refreshing! **Please don't change who you are**."

(In my mind: from Adam to Nora)
<u>Enduring a paralyzing love</u>

The year was nineteen thirty-six
The entire empire was in a fix
The king fell dangerously in love
But the affair was a forbidden love

The empire felt the power of a love cyclone
That violently shook the British throne
But the king could only hear her love song
He was in too deep, her love was too strong

The fiery storm was too much to withstand
He tried, but his subjects did not understand
The king succumbed to his loving heart
He abdicated the throne for his sweetheart
He reigned for less than a year
He went with Wallis Simpson, his dear
And were married for thirty-five years

Paralyzing love makes everything disappear
Except the one you truly love, your dear
It is the only love in the atmosphere
You see and smell love everywhere
You really wished you had a clone
So you can talk non-stop on the phone

Now, I clearly understand King Edward VIII's decision
To go with a divorcee rather than ruling his kingdom
It was due to a paralyzing love
A feeling that is second to none

This type of love is paralyzing
But it is sweet, not demoralizing
Although it turns your world upside down
But you are happy and don't feel down

My love, if only you are fully in the know
You will be shocked to your bone marrow

I know that you really don't know
What I am prepared to give up for your love
Because you are the one that I truly love
And my love for you...... is a paralyzing love!

The message from Adam to Nora: "I love you with my heart, my body and my soul. **Please see me like I see you for a change**."

Part One

Changing Course:
The story of Adam

Part One: Section One:
Who is getting married?

"What!" Adam remarked, quite unable to believe his eyes. He closed his eyes immediately just in case he was having a visual hallucination. He shook his head vigorously for unknown reasons. It is unclear if that maneuver clears the human brain or not. It was a reflex action of some sort. Well, dogs do shake their bodies vigorously to expel any unwanted water from their fur after a bath. The goal was simple though. He wanted to be jolted back to reality and be comforted that what he just saw on Facebook was not true. He opened his eyes. Alas! The message was still there. Adam could not control himself. He pressed the power button of his laptop computer and shut it down without signing off his Facebook log in. He got up from his chair and paced for a few minutes in his bedroom. He made a fist with his right hand and punched his left palm a few times. It was as if he was trying to wake up from a nightmare. He pinched himself just to make sure that he could feel pain and have another confirmatory sensorium that he was not asleep and what he just read was real.

"Yes, it was real. Yes, it was for real," a soft voice in his head reassured him. However, a more opinionated and dominant voice rejected the claim. "No! It cannot be," it said.

Suddenly, Adam felt the urge to use the bathroom. He

quickly dashed into the bathroom in his master's suite and sat on the toilet seat, but nothing happened. After sitting down brooding on the toilet seat in total shock for about five minutes, he got up, dressed up, washed his hands and left the bathroom.

Adam went straight to the chair in his bedroom and sat down. His hands were trembling slightly from a bad mixture of anger and anxiety. He reopened his laptop. He pressed the power button for a couple of seconds to turn it back on. After a few seconds of waiting for the laptop computer to fully boot up which felt like eternity to Adam, he yelled "shut up!" to the computer screen and then mumbled to himself, 'shut down properly my foot!'. Adam was responding in anger to the message from his computer during the rebooting process which stated that 'Windows did not shut down properly.'

Adam quickly logged back into Facebook and there it was again. The painful message which shattered his dreams and broke his heart. It was the picture of Nora flashing her engagement ring and her friends congratulating her in advance of her wedding the following week. "Is Nora really getting married in 7 days?" Adam asked himself. He still could not believe his eyes. Even though it has been three months since he last had contact with her, he still could not believe that Nora was getting married to that spoiled brat the following week. Apparently, they had their engagement about four weeks earlier. Adam was not informed by anybody. He was totally in the dark. He had not checked Nora's Facebook page since their chance encounter when he bumped into her at the Alexandria mall three months previously. He had mailed a birthday card to her home on her twenty-fourth birthday just a few weeks previously. Of course, he did not get a call back as usual. He tried to reason why he was placed in information blackout, but nothing seemed to make any sense. It would have been dignifying if Nora or even somebody else from Nora's family had informed him. "Did Nora really choose to marry that little brat?" Adam asked himself again as if he needed another confirmation. He felt that he was mistreated by Nora and her family. Norma also could have given him a call too. After all she was aware of his love for Nora and his intention to marry her sister. He wondered if Norma was under communication embargo too. Adam picked up his cellphone to call Nora. However, he changed his mind as he was about to press number nine continuously to call her. He had called her several times and texted her many times in the last two months without any call back or response anyway. So, there was no use in calling her for the umpteenth time. Adam shook his head as per the irony of his life that has just unfolded. He had set up his phone so that Nora was always on his speed dial number nine and had a composition to honor the decision to save her number on his speed dial number nine.

Speed dial: Number nine

You are my number nine
Not just because you are fine
And I want you to be mine
Or because I will like us to dine
Or move up together on an incline
To lovingly touch the sky

You are my number nine
You are on my speed dial number nine
Because nine is the starting number
For 9-1-1, the emergency number

So that if I have an emergency
And I cannot make it to the emergency room
If I can only dial nine
Rather than the full 9-1-1
I will crave to remind you
I will desire to inform you
I will want to tell you
One last time…
…How much I love you

I love you
I will always love you
I will love you forever and ever

Yes, I will want your voice
To be the last voice I hear
As I return home to my Lord

Darling, don't ever doubt my love for you.

Unfortunately, now she is gone but she is still on speed dial number nine. Adam sunk his head into his hands as the screen of his computer turned dark due to an extended period of inactivity. He had been staring at the screen with activities occurring only in his head. Of course, the computer did not know that his brain was not inactive. It was active in being shocked to the core. It was active in nursing bruised ego. It was active in trying to make sense of dashed hopes. It was active in trying not to cry from a deep sense of loss, the unbearable hurt from loss of love.

So much for his love for her! So much for his conviction that they belong together! This was his birthday message to Nora in the card he sent her a short while ago. How wrong he was! Adam sighed in despair.

"Life is an irony" Adam remarked to himself as he picked up a piece of paper that fell from his table to the floor. He looked at the piece of paper and shook his head. He had jotted a few lines of love message on this paper a few hours earlier. He had decided to break his self-imposed retreat from Nora by sending her this heartfelt message to her. That was why he was using his laptop computer in the first place. However, his longing for Nora was what made him checked her on Facebook at that moment. He wanted to relish is his recall of his love for her prior to sending her the email he intended. A part of him felt happy that he had not sent the message. It would have been very awkward and embarrassing to him. He shook his head and felt that he was saved by the Facebook bell. No doubt, if he had sent the message and somebody else ended up reading his poem, the person would conclude wrongly that he must have been stalking Nora who has been engaged to marry somebody else. However, that conclusion would have been very wrong. Adam looked at the piece of paper and read the note to himself.

"Nora my love:

<u>Thriving in my travails</u>

No mountain is too high
For me to climb
No river is too long
For me to swim
No ocean is too deep
For me to traverse
No desert is too hot
For me to cross

No obstacle is too difficult
For me to overcome
To reach you my darling
To see your lovely eyes.

I am coming to you
I am coming for you
I want to be with you

I love you.

Adam felt dejected. The poem had no meaning anymore. Nora is gone! "I guess my last message to her was destined to be the final message of love from me to her," Adam finally spoke aloud to himself trying to resign to fate.

A part of him wished Nora well, but no part of him could ever wish Richard well. He genuinely felt that he had been robbed of his love by wealth. He tried to rationalize why he should be happy for them as a couple, but no reasoning or explanation or rationalization made sense. The thought of the card he sent to Nora a few weeks earlier flashed through his mind bringing him a smile which quickly turned into a frown.

<u>A birthday message to the most special lady in the world.</u>

If Galileo Galilei, Isaac Newton, Archimedes, Albert Einstein, Socrates and Avicenna were to evaluate our situation individually or collectively,

It is very obvious
It is very clear
It is very apparent that....

No matter the formulae they use
No matter the assumptions they make
No matter the calculations they perform
No matter the types and numbers of graphs they draw
No matter the statistical models they build

They will come to the same conclusion that:

I TRULY LOVE YOU Nora!
And I will always be here for you
And I will always be there for you.

Happy birthday to you my love.
Many happy returns.

However, quite unknown to Adam, Nora never got the card. When the card arrived in the mail, her mum, Zinnia, took the card on seeing that it was from Adam. She opened the card, read it and tore it. Zinnia remarked that these smart people Adam mentioned will get an error message with their calculations if they have an illusion that Nora will ever marry Adam.

Adam looked at the picture of Nora again. The ring she was flashing made him feel sick to his stomach. He enlarged the image to get more information about the ring. He did not quite figure out anything on looking at the enlarged picture. It only looked "very expensive" which further infuriated Adam. He continued to ask himself several questions with all of them beginning with "why?" Unfortunately, there were no satisfactory answers. Maybe it was just him who did not know the answers, but those who knew the answers were not talking to him about the answers.

After a few minutes of sinking his head onto his folded hands, he spoke aloud, "what exactly made Richard a better candidate for Nora than me?" He asked himself with his inner being answering the question. His mind gave him a distasteful answer that Richard was the final choice of Nora. Her family also preferred Richard for obvious reasons. Richard is younger, his parents have a lot of money and he is an only child… but Adam's mind quickly added, "but he is a putrid rotten spoiled brat!" in his spirited attempt to halt his self-abasement.

"Did my age work against me?" Adam asked himself after a few seconds, when his attempt to use deep breathing exercise to bring him a much-needed calmness failed woefully. He recalled his conversation with Ray and Kamal on the subject matter previously.

Adam had remarked, "there should be a law that permits a mature older man to marry a younger woman if he is up to it."

"There is no law against it. There is no restriction of the age of marriage once you are not considered to be a minor," Ray had replied.

"Who is a minor in terms of marriage?" Adam sought clarification.

"It varies by states," Ray explained. "In general, you have to be eighteen before you are no longer considered to be a minor for the purpose of marriage. That means anybody older than eighteen can get married without parental consent. However, it is part of the societal norm to seek parental consent before marriage, especially for the first marriage."

"Eighteen, hey?" Kamal remarked.

"And what about it?" Ray questioned.

Kamal shrugged his shoulders and continued "but teenagers under eighteen can go and get free condoms in hospitals and outreach STD clinics and HIV prevention centers."

"That is for disease prevention," Adam responded.

"But they are not allowed to get married, but they are sanctioned to savor the forbidden fruit?" Kamal queried.

"Well, I know it sounds hypocritical…."

"No! It is hypocritical. I think if we would give tacit approval for young folks to dance between the sheets, we might as well allow them to actually get married, be committed to it and be responsible for the products of such engagements," Kamal emphasized his point.

"I completely understand your point," Ray agreed. "In any case, I don't make laws. For the older folks though, there is no restriction based on age. A man can marry a younger or older woman as he pleases and vice versa. So, a ninety-year old man can marry a twenty-year old lady and a ninety-year old lady can marry a twenty-year old man."

"You are kidding, right?" Kamal inquired a joking manner.

"I am serious," Ray affirmed.

"You really think a ninety-year old woman can marry a twenty-year old young, virile, agile, hormone-raging man-bull in his prime?"

"Yes," Ray replied.

"And you are not insane?" Kamal pressed on.

"Ray is definitely insane," Adam chimed in with his conclusion.

"Of course not. I am definitely not insane. She may be a dynamite you know," Ray giggled while responding.

"Look guys! At ninety, I don't care if you are a man or woman, if you call yourself a dynamite and marry a twenty-year old, it means you want to explode. Any twenty-year old who married a ninety-year old should be charged with elderly abuse. End of story!" Adam concluded.

"Look at who is criticizing an explosion of love! Sorry, I mean explosion from love… as in Ka-boom!!!" Kamal remarked as he pointed to Adam. "Aren't you a heartbeat from turning ninety and you want to marry the twenty-year old dynamic, dynamite, dynamo Nova who is constantly causing nova explosions of love in your about-to-be-broken heart?" Kamal made air quotes while saying "about-to-be-broken heart" to Adam.

Kamal and Ray busted into laughter, but Adam frowned.

"It is not funny!" Adam remarked.

"Yes, we know. Why do you think we are trying to bring you from your fantasy world into reality?" Kamal asked in jest. "You behave as if you are a simple guy."

"Yes, I am simple," Adam snarled.

"Complicated," Kamal remarked.

"Simple," Adam reiterated.

"Complicated," Kamal restated.

"Simple," Adam reemphasized.

"Unnecessarily complicated," Kamal opined.

"Very simple," Adam fought back.

"Simply complicated," Kamal pressed further.

"Non-complicatedly simple," Adam clarified.

"Simply very complicated," Kamal disagreed.

"Simply simple," Adam affirmed.

"Why are you guys still stuck in your teenage years?" Ray asked Adam and Kamal a rhetorical question.

"It is this genius who does not know the difference between men and women relative to advancing ages," Adam remarked.

"And you know?" Kamal asked with sarcasm.

"Of course, I do," Adam responded. "I am a physician, remember?"

"Yea. You are indeed a less-than below-average physician who does not know that heart attack is like a shark attack.....you do everything you can..... to avoid them!" Kamal criticized.

Ray held the right hand of Adam to urge him to look away from Kamal. "Don't mind him. Tell me the difference you had in mind."

Adam shot a disappointing look at Kamal and faced Ray. He then remarked, "an eighteen-year-old babe is *waiting to inhale*. She is about to start the best journey of her life. She is about to experience what her mother warned her about. A forty-year-old lady is *waiting to exhale*. She is just about to pass her prime. She is slowly coming to the twilight of the most engaging part of....you know.... with that ultimate primary responsibility..... which was making her drive her husband crazy. However, a sixty-five-year-old woman is *waiting to explode*. She has been there and done that already. Nothing excites her anymore. She is about to enter the phase of loneliness if she did not create a supportive milieu for herself when she was younger. This becomes the phase of regrets if she did not get her priorities right in terms of taking care of her husband, raising her children well, having grand-children, having resources to retire on, having a community of friends, support groups, and volunteering in the community. For some women, this is the sad phase when it finally dawns on them that their priorities should have been to have a great relationship with their husbands. In this phase, the need of the man for hanky-panky that makes him hanker after her and be putting up with her issues would have gone down substantially. He will still not be interested in 'holding hands' that leads to nowhere. Moreover, he may be dead already anyway..."

"You are a real prophet of doom!" Kamal interjected.

Adam simply ignored him.

"What about men?" Ray asked Adam.

"An eighteen-year-old man is just waiting. He is not inhaling anything yet. He doesn't even know what inhaling means. Sure, his hormones are raging like el-toro the bull, but it is nothing but brute force with little sense. It is much worse nowadays when boys are spoiled rotten. They just sit down in their rooms playing video games all day long while the girls are busy working. They are very irresponsible because their mothers spoiled them by not making them do house chores. Sometimes, they are so completely useless that they bring their dirty laundry from college for their mothers to wash at home.

"You must really be in a very bad mood," Kamal suggested.

"Nope. I am just calling a spade a shovel," Adam responded.

"Whatever!" Kamal resigned.

"I am listening to your analogy, Dr. Analyst," Ray chimed in for Adam to continue.

"A 40-year-old man has arrived. He is full of wisdom and well accomplished. Unfortunately, the chicks that he wants would have started running away from him with the erroneous belief that he is too old," Adam regretted.

"I actually agree with you there....you know.. except the part where you gave the impression that you are full of wisdom. I mean it is obvious that you were talking about yourself here, right?" Kamal opined.

"Must you be annoying all the time? I think you should

call your shrink on his hotline to double the dose of your medicine or better still, he should change it to something stronger," Adam responded to Kamal.

"Ignore him please. I am enjoying your bogus analysis. Please continue," Ray weighed into the conversation.

"Anyway, for a 65-year-old man, hmmm! Well, let us just say that he is lucky to have made it thus far from occupational hazards and marital problems. He is finally in cruise control. He takes stock and start regretting all those decisions he did not make at the right time that would have served him well now. He gradually comes to terms that he does not have the same strength or earning power or new prospects at this important phase of his life."

"Adam my friend. My good friend. My great friend." Kamal expressed with a smirk. "I am totally in agreement with you that you will suddenly turn into the sixty-five-year-old you just described after Aneida marries somebody else."

"With a statement like that, I am definitely not your friend, Kamal. How and where did our path crossed anyway?" Adam asked without expecting any answer.

Adam snapped back into the moment and mused to himself "it is amazing that no matter your age, you relate to people based on how old they were, and you were, when you first met them. You act like kids to those you met when you were kids and act maturely for those you met as adults."

This is indeed the new reality. Although it is a totally different reality from what Kamal was warning him about. Kamal's doomsday heartbreak reality was far better than this one in Adam's opinion. At least, he would have married his true love in that reality even if he ends up with *a loving heart attack*. Sadly, in this current reality, his true love was snatched from him because of age and wealth discrimination. This is surely *a bad heart attack*. Adam shook his head in sadness. He recalled that the conversation with the guys about him having a heart attack over Nora bothered him a bit. However, his love for Nora easily dwarfed any concern. He was very hopeful that things will work out eventually between him and Nora. He was convinced that his love for Nora will win out in the end. Later that evening, he sent her a text message emphasizing to Nora that his love for her is evergreen and everlasting.

Now, that future is gone! Adam dejectedly went to lay down on the bed and starred at the ceiling. The reality that Nora is marrying Richard continued to feel like a nightmare. He continued to query why nobody told him about the engagement and the planned wedding. He concluded that Nora's family must not have told him because they did not want him to attend the wedding. However, a part of him tried to convince him to attend the wedding in order to get some closure but a voice of reasoning appealed to him not to do so because it makes no sense to go to the wedding uninvited. The fact is that Nora has crossed 'the point of no return.'

"What is the use in going to the wedding?" Adam asked himself. He dared not get there and say that he does not want the couple to be married because he thinks that he is more deserving of her hands or that he is in love with her. The attendees will think that he has gone raving mad and he should be shot with a tranquilizer and admitted to a psychiatry ward. Moreover, what if he shows up and they denied him entrance because he will have no wedding invitation card? That would be more embarrassing to him. Besides, he is not even sure how he will handle watching the lady he described as his soulmate being married to somebody else!

"I can't. Definitely, I can't," Adam replied to himself when he asked himself how he will handle the 'now you may kiss the bride segment?'

Adam concluded that attending the wedding will be too demoralizing for him. He was already feeling heartbroken knowing that he has lost the hands of Nora. Definitely, watching her kiss another guy will make him go bonkers. It was better for him not to attend Nora's wedding. Now, he felt that everybody did him a favor by not telling him about the planned wedding.

Adam went to bed that night feeling disappointed. He felt

robbed and was emotionally hurt. A voice of reason in his head reminded him of the popular statement: "if you love something, you should let it go. If it comes back to you, then it is yours forever, but if it doesn't, it was never meant to be." Adam countered angrily at such a thought calling it stupid and ridiculous and totally not applicable to his love for Nora. Even though he was alone in his bedroom, Adam could not help speaking to himself loudly, "what an arrant nonsense! What is the meaning of ....if she comes back? What rubbish will that be? After she is divorced? Nonsense!"

After about thirty minutes of tossing and turning on the bed trying desperately to forget the sadness that was enveloping him like a thick putrid fog, Adam conjured up a smiling image of Nora in his head and his heart softly wished her well. He certainly would have preferred for him to be her husband. Well, it was not meant to be.

Unknown to Adam, at the time that he was having his emotional crises of love, Nora was tossing and turning in bed unable to sleep too. She was asking herself if she was making the right decision in going through with the planned wedding. A part of her felt that she was making a grave mistake by marrying Richard, but what can she do? She does not want to break her mother's heart. Her marriage meant a lot to her mum. Nora sighed when she asked herself a question without a definite answer: "who is this marriage for?"

The answer was not so simple to Nora. Yes, she is the one getting a wedding ring and a marriage certificate. However, it is conceivable that it may be taking place for her mother, Zinnia who is happy to be getting her daughter married into a high society. Nonetheless, it is arguable that it was taking place for Richard's mum who wanted to force the hands of Richard into settling down. Hence, the plan to make him marry a beautiful decent girl so that he can settle down and stop being a Casanova.

"I wonder what Adam is doing now!" Nora expressed loudly as she turned to her left side on the bed and covered her face with the sheet.

Part One: Section Two:
Who got married?

"Breakfast is ready," Adam shouted, calling his children to the dining table. Sarah came immediately. She was up already. She just stayed in her room. She could smell the aroma of pancake her dad was making. She just did not realize that many of the pancakes were burnt because he was frequently absent-minded even though he was standing in the kitchen next to the stove. He was still trying to make sense of the enveloping nightmare of the idea that Nora is getting married to Richard in less than a week. It was still hard for him to believe.

Adam served Sarah her pancakes and scrambled eggs as Sheriff came down to the dining table. After the breakfast was over, Sheriff left the table almost as quickly as he came down from his room upstairs, but Sarah remained behind. She sat quietly just looking on at nothing in particular. This was unusual and Adam knew immediately that something was wrong. The last time she exhibited this sort of behavior was when she had her period a few months ago and thought she had injured herself unknowingly. Adam was initially confused. Even though he is a physician, he was initially puzzled and did not know how best to address the issue with Sarah. In the end, he managed to get through with it, but it was a very awkward conversation. Adam wished Eva was alive and he was almost moved to tears when he remembered his late wife. Adam recognized that he would not have had to deal with that situation if Eva, his wife and Sarah's mother, had been alive. The thought of the challenges of that day gave him goosebumps as he recalled going to the superstore to buy female hygiene products. He felt embarrassed as he looked at the shelves to find rows and rows of sanitary towels of different costs with different claims of absorbency and odor protection. Some brands also claimed to have wings which did not make any sense to Adam. "Why will wings be needed in a sanitary towel when there is no flying involved?" Adam asked himself. The only function of a sanitary towel is to absorb and contain blood and prevent leaks. A sanitary towel with sky blue cover caught his attention. It had "prevents leaks from heavy periods" written on it.

"What is a heavy period? Five pounds? Ten pounds?" Adam asked himself while shaking his head. "These companies just know how to convince women to waste their husbands' money in buying things they really don't need," he concluded.

In the end, he just picked a cheaper brand that also has 'heavy' written on it without fully understanding what that really meant. He reasoned that heavy containment will be better than light containment. That was good enough. He felt very shy when he put the packets of sanitary towels on his cart. He felt as if other shoppers were looking at him in a creepy manner. So, he decided to buy some loaves of bread to cover up the sanitary towels from view. When he reached the checkout counter, the lady cashier looked at him smiling lovingly and admiringly after she saw that he bought sanitary towels. Every time she scanned an item and put it in a plastic bag, she would look at Adam with an appreciative inviting smile. Her inviting smile made Adam feel very creepy.

Fortunately for him, the sanitary towel brand he bought did the job very well. He has stuck with that brand for Sarah since then. That experience had increased the mental urgency that Adam had in getting married again. Unfortunately, Nora, the *object* of his *objective* is now going to be married to someone else. This putrid thought made his fork drop from his hand unknowingly.

"Dad," Sarah interrupted Adam in his thought.

"Yes, my dear," he responded.

"I need something."

"Okay. What is it?"

"It is a female thing."

"Does this 'female thing' has a name?" Adam asked while making air quotes on saying female thing.

"Em.. em..em… it is something ladies wear."

"Ladies wear a lot of things. They never stop wearing things. Please don't get me started. Ladies will wear wears they love until it is worn and worn out. I mean ladies will…"

"Okay dad," Sarah interjected. "I need a bra." Sarah said softly being shy.

"Bra? Bra?" Adam repeated as if he was unsure what he heard. "What made you think you need bra?" He asked her while looking at her.

"Dad, I know," Sarah replied as she lowered her head to hide her chest on the table.

"How old are you that you think you need a bra?"

"It is not by age dad."

"Well, you are about the same height as your mum now. You can go to our bedroom, try her bras and see which ones fit you."

"Seriously? That is not funny dad."

"What! Nobody else in this house can wear them."

"Hmmm!!!," Sarah grumbled.

"Ok, fine. We will go to the mall," Adam surrendered.

The thought of going to buy bra for Sarah made Adam uncomfortable and brought back memories of when he had to buy sanitary towel as an emergency. He really felt the need for a wife now more than ever. At least, any woman will be good enough to help Sarah with these feminine things.

"This is so hard," Adam said to himself while trying to force a fake smile so that Sarah will not feel bad. "Being a single dad is really difficult. I think single mothers have it a lot easier."

Author's note: Is it really easier to be a single mum?

Adam continued to argue in his mind that it is a lot harder to be a single dad than to be a single mum. Nobody gives you any slack for being a single dad, but the society tends to give certain unquantifiable pity to single mums without any consideration for what actually happened that led to the single parenthood. The protagonist part of Adam's mind argued that for a man to be a single dad, he is most likely a widower like him which means that he has already suffered a major loss. If he was a divorcee and he ended up with the children as a single dad, he must have suffered greatly in the hands of the wife. That would be the only reason why he ended up with the children. It is well known that, by default, children tend to be with their mother after divorce. On the other hand, a woman can have a child out of wedlock whether through natural or artificial conception to become a single mum. It may even be that she kicked her husband out of the house. Women sometimes listen to other women who are envious of them and push them into ruining their marriages over trifles until the good, or the okay, or the fair guy is gone. Later, when the dust has settled, they then settle for anyone and they keep falling victim to vultures. The antagonist in Adam's mind countered that sometimes, a good woman just ends up with a horrible man and becoming a single mum is the better option.

Later in the morning, Adam and Sarah made it to the "Ladies" section in the Super Megastore, but he had no clue about how to go about their father-daughter quest for an initiation bra. The display of many models wearing only bra and underwear to advertise products made him very uncomfortable. He really wanted to get out of the "Ladies" section as fast as he could.

"Sarah."

"Yes, dad."

"Go ahead and pick the ones you want."

"I don't know which ones to get, dad."

"O my God!" Adam exclaimed throwing his hands in the air out of frustration.

Adam approached the attendant in charge of the changing room to ask for help. The attendant started explaining the nomenclature of bra to Adam in terms of straps, cup, band, gore, underwires, and hooks. Adam was just nodding his head without any comprehension of what the lady was talking about. By the time she got to explaining the full cup, demi cup and something called balcony or balconette with A, B and D classification of some sort with some even numbers, Adam was totally lost. He was unsure if the lady skipped C while mentioning A, B, C, D, but he thought he heard her say something DD or DDD when he was expecting E, F, G, H. It was very confusing.

Suddenly, Adam mustered the confidence to actually ask for more help rather than pretending that he understood what the attendant was talking about.

"Sorry Miss…" Adam tried to address the attendant.

"Branca. You can call me Branca," she replied.

"Branca, thank you very much for all the explanation but could you please assist me with helping her pick what she actually needs?"

"I am sorry sir, but I can't leave this post at this time because I have clients who are in the fitting rooms."

"Thank you very much," Adam responded while shaking his head. The only thing he knew about bra was unhooking it and taking it off Eva, his now deceased wife. Now, he wished he knew a lot more. He thought of going to the coffee shop inside the store for a late morning coffee with *banana nut muffin*. He thought this was befitting because his daughter will soon be driving him *nuts* from her female needs and he does not want to go *bananas*.

Adam bent down to be at an eye-level with Sarah. He put his hands on her shoulders and remarked, "I guess we will have to wait a bit for some assistance."

As if by a stroke of luck, a lady shopping in another isle heard the voice of a desperate father and came nearer because the voice was very familiar. She smiled at Adam and asked him, "how may I be of help?"

Adam looked up and saw the lady who was offering to help him and his daughter. His being came alive, his face glowed with happiness and he beamed with smiles on recognizing her.

"Aneida! I am so glad to see you. I am so sorry. I really have in mind to return your phone call last month. I have been very busy."

Aneida raised her hand and nodded to signify that it was okay. She smiled at Sarah.

Adam introduced Sarah to Aneida and vice versa and referred to Aneida as a special friend.

"Come with me young woman!" Aneida remarked to Sarah who was just glad to have been rescued from her clueless father.

"I will be waiting for you ladies in the electronics section," Adam informed them sighing relief.

Sarah and Aneida went to get a shopping cart. With Aneida as a willing accomplice, Sarah seized the opportunity to buy things beyond the initiation bra she came to the store for. In addition to six bras, she took sanitary towels, leggings, camisoles, many underwear, socks, a pair of running shoes, a pair of black platform wedge heel shoes and a pair of red closed toe wedge heel pumps in her shopping cart.

Sarah was happy to have gotten everything she wanted, and she was so sure that daddy will not say "No" to her items in the presence of this nice stranger who helped him. She decided to sweeten the deal by getting three vanilla ice cream cones with peanut toppings for herself, Aneida and her father. The goal of the ice cream cones was simple. For her dad, it was to 'bribe' him so that he won't say "*no*" to the other items she bought. For Aneida, it was to thank her for helping her. For Sarah, she just wanted to eat the ice cream. The ice cream was too tempting. She felt as if the brightly colored ice cream display was inviting her and screaming her name loudly from the freezer in the middle of the isle as she was making her way to the electronic section to meet her dad for his credit card.

"Dad!, Dad!!" Sarah shouted with excitement as she and Aneida made it to the electronic section where Adam was playing a video game on a demo console in the store.

"Yes Sarah," Adam replied with a smile of appreciation as he looked at Aneida. "Thank you very much, Aneida. I really appreciate your help."

At that juncture, Sarah handed her dad his ice cream cone and offered one to Aneida who refused it.

"Please Aneida! Please take it. It is her way of saying *'thank you'* to you," Adam chimed in. Aneida then accepted the ice cream cone gift and thanked Sarah for her kind gesture.

"Let's go dad," Sarah commanded as she started making her way to the checkout lane.

"Wait, wait, wait!" Adam exclaimed as his eyes caught the pair of red closed toe wedge heel pumps in the shopping cart. "How many things did you buy?"

"Daaaaaad," Sarah responded with a tone that signify "please."

Adam looked at Aneida who simply smiled and shrugged her shoulders.

Sarah seized the moment and held her father's right hand dragging him to the checkout lane.

"How old are you that you want to wear high heels? What do you need high heels for?" Adam asked as he was being pulled by his daughter.

"These heels were designed for teenagers, dad." Sarah replied as she let go of Adam's hand so that she could push the shopping cart with both hands.

Adam simply shook his head and followed her. The feeling of relief on Sarah's face when a woman decided to help her with her needs was priceless. The only thing she really needed from her father was his credit card. After all, if her mum had been alive, he would never have heard anything about Sarah needing a bra. He looked at Aneida and remarked "indeed, the father has his role and the mother has her role, both are truly complementary."

"I agree," Aneida responded with a smile.

Adam wondered why the society seems to be hell-bent on making a woman what she is not supposed to be...... as a he-woman or a she-man. In contrast, nobody will encourage a man to become a lady. "A *'man-lady'* would really be a *'malady,'* Adam mused to himself. It is not natural.

They made their way to the checkout lane. Adam insisted on paying for Aneida's items too. He paid for all the items picked by Sarah.

"Thank you very much Aneida. I really appreciate your helping me out."

"My pleasure."

"What is your plan for next weekend?" Adam asked Aneida.

"I am free on Saturday, but I have a morning shift on Sunday."

"Perfect!" Adam exclaimed. "We could have a picnic together if you would like to. Sarah would surely want to see you again. I will bring her and her brother, Sheriff to meet Evelyn and Ben. We can meet for lunch around noon at Great Friendship park in New Carrollton...that is...if this is okay with you."

"Er,,,er...well, I guess it is fine," Aneida mustered an acceptance of the invitation. She then bid Adam and Sarah farewell.

"Who is she.... really, dad?" Sarah asked Adam.

"What did you mean?" Adam replied with a question.

"I saw the look in your eyes ...I mean...the way.... you looked at her..."

"What way did I look at her?" Adam interrupted Sarah.

"I know what I saw...and you were still turning your head to look at her after she left...."

"Mind your own business...little miss busybody!" Adam responded as he playfully pushed Sarah on her left shoulder.

"Is she going to be our step-mum?" Sarah asked undeterred.

"What!" Adam exclaimed. "What are you talking about?"

"I think you like her."

"Hmmm!"

"All I am saying is that she is nice, and I think she likes you too."

"And what made you think she likes me?" Adam became curious as they walked to the car in the parking lot.

"From the way she talked about you when we were shopping."

"What did she say?" Adam inquired more as he put on his seatbelt.

"She asked me if my brother and I are treating you well and taking good care of you. I thought she should have asked the question the other way around by asking if you were taking good care of us. Then, she said that you are a nice person."

"Hmmm!" Adam sighed again.

"What?"

"Nothing," Adam responded.

"I think you like her too. After all, you just asked her out."

"And you figured that out…… all by yourself?" Adam chuckled.

"Dad. I am not a kid anymore. I am almost thirteen."

"Great! Another teenage expert in the house. Now, I am really in trouble."

"Hmmm!" Sarah sighed.

As they drove back home, Adam could not help reflecting on his marital life quest as it was unfolding before his very eyes. It was as if the choice has been made for him. After all, there is no doubt in his mind anymore that Nora is gone. Not just that he is left with Aneida at this point, but he is also coming to realize that Aneida is not a bad choice at all. It was just that he loves Nora more than he loves Aneida. It was not that he did not have feelings for Aneida. However, the fact that Sarah likes her already will even make family integration a lot easier. It is well known that while men and women can destroy family bonds, women are really the glue that hold families together. Therefore, a situation where the ladies like one another before the family integration is the best scenario and fortuitously, that seems to be what was happening to his family and Aneida's family. Typically, the men in the family integration will fall in line easily. It is always very easy for men to find common grounds than women, Adam wondered why. "I guess it is because women are always very complicated," Adam reasoned to himself.

The journey home was uneventful. Adam went straight to his bedroom while Sarah busied herself with trying on her new apparels and her high heels shoes. She paraded herself in front of the mirror endlessly as if she was practicing how to walk on the red carpet while attending the Oscars.

"Wow!" Adam exclaimed loudly and he jumped on his

bed starring at the ceiling. Now, he felt happy that Sarah had forced him to go to the mall with her to shop for bra which has now opened his eyes and his heart for Aneida.

"Wow!" He exclaimed again still unable to believe how fast things seems to be moving. Now, he and his children are now going to meet Aneida and her children. Adam reflected on the numerous condemnation he had hurled at Aneida's candidacy during his conversations with Ray and Kamal. He recalled a particular discussion in which he told the guys about an infomercial about a dietary supplement, *Timeless Bliss*. In the advertisement, women were classified in a continuum of excitement to men in a so-called *Desirability Factor*. The lady infomercial presenter likened women to the season. She explained that when ladies reach maturity that are like fresh spring and rapidly evolve into the desirable hot summer where they stay until their leaves of life which defines them as trees begin to fall in the Fall. By menopause, they are in the cold winter when they would have lost the warm and tender touch that men desire. She argued that her product will prolong the summer for all women, delay the Fall and make winter a lot more tolerable. Although the product with this great claim was just a supplement from an unknown tree, the presenter did not present any scientific basis for the claims. Unfortunately, these products are not regulated by the Food and Drug Administration (FDA). Unsuspecting people take them hoping for a miracle while taking placebo. That was Adam's conclusion when he watched the infomercial. He had watched it while working late that night on his computer when he was preparing a lecture for nursing students. However, when he was relating it to his buddies, he focused on the bogus classification of when women are in season claiming that Nora is hot summer and Aneida is in the Fall, very close to winter. The classification of women like a continuum of season and Adam's take on Nora and Aneida had Kamal exasperated.

"You and that infomercial presenter are crazy," Kamal yelled. "Maybe you should get her number and marry her instead."

Adam ignored him and continued. "The next infomercial

was selling another beauty product in form of a cream and that classified ladies as cool morning, hot prime, warm twilight and cold night. The product being sold was likened to the elusive mythical 'fountain of youth' and it was supposed to keep every woman in hot prime."

"Did you buy some of the magic cream for your dream wife?" Kamal mocked Adam.

"If I was interested in those fake products, I would rather buy the one that stated that the supplement will make the user to be forever young, forever prime, forever hot and forever fresh."

Kamal shook his head in amazement wondering why Adam behaves as if his head is completely empty.

"Why do these products always target women and sell fake products which promise to deliver a live unicorn to their bedrooms?" Ray inquired.

"But they target men too," Kamal corrected him.

"How?" Ray pressed further.

"What about those infomercials that target men urging them to buy some stupid supplements that will make them bulk up and look like the incredible Hulk claiming that it will let them be able to go twelve rounds every night with their wives?" Kamal retorted.

"Relax man!" Ray responded. "Why are you so feisty? Have you tried them before, and they did not deliver what they promised?"

"Never!" Kamal responded sharply. "I put *man* in *manly*. So, I don't need them. Have you tried them?" Kamal questioned Ray with sarcasm.

"C'mon man! I have not used anything right now and Desiree could not cope. I am an all-natural, all-organic macho-man with an undeniable machismo. That is why Desiree is already on her knees. What do you think will happen if I now use a 'performance enhancing drug?'" Ray asked Kamal while making air quotes on mentioning performance enhancing drug.

Kamal and Adam busted into laughter.

"She will probably take her kids, run to NASA, and board a space shuttle on a one-way ticket to Saturn or Neptune. She will physically run out of this world!" Ray concluded as he joined in the laughter.

> **Author's note:** To my lady readers, I do apologize (smile). Sorry. It is a guy thing. Everyman thinks that he is God's gift to his wife...even the under-performing ones! So, no need to burst their bubbles.

"I still don't understand why people will play on the emotion of others just to make money through these stupid infomercials," Kamal expressed his frustration.

"Well, they play on the different emotions for men and women. Every woman wants to feel beautiful and every man wants to feel strong," Ray explained.

"I believe all women are beautiful and all men are strong," Kamal opined.

"Hmmm! That would be the Lake Wobegon Effect from Garrison Keillor's A Prairie Home Companion," Adam suggested.

"Really? Okay. I stand corrected. All women are beautiful, and all men are strong except Adam Gray. He is on Island Wobegon, all by himself," Kamal remarked chuckling.

"You are nuts!" Adam fought back.

"You are the one that is not getting your priorities right. You are drunk on optimism juice thinking that there is a world in which Zinnia the plant will allow you to marry Nova. You are forgetting that Nova is a decent parent-respecting young lady who is never going to elope with you. So, your chances of marrying her is zero. Just to make it clearer to you, I mean a big fat zero," Kamal expressed with stern voice.

"You make it sound as if the size of zero matters!" Adam countered. "It only shows that you are not as smart as you think."

"All I know is that you need to see a better shrink so that he can double the dose of your reality medication because whatever your druid is brewing now is not working!" Kamal retorted.

"Stop worrying yourself, my self-appointed fake counselor," Adam remarked while facing Kamal. "I hereby appoint you as my undertaker. If I die from having a great, fulfilling, real life with Nora, let the epitaph on my tombstone read 'To the glory of God, he died fulfilling his duty as a very happy man.'"

Kamal shook his head and threw his hands up in surrender.

Adam smiled as he put his hands underneath his pillow as his brain came back to the present. He wondered what Kamal would say to him with the current development that he will actually give the relationship with Aneida a real chance. "Kamal would laugh until he passes out," Adam expressed to himself.

Adam spent the week wondering what to bring to the lunch get-together with Aneida and her children. He was unsure what to buy for Aneida and her children as gifts. Ben is now seventeen years old and Evelyn is already thirteen years old. Their ages are in the same range as his children. His son, Sheriff, is fifteen years old and Sarah is almost 13 years old too. In the end, he got a fruit basket, chicken and turkey wraps, dinner rolls and hummus from the *Grocer Store*. He got a heart shaped cheesecake for dessert and Sparkling Apple Cider Juice for drinks. He got a beautiful cashmere scarf for Aneida and athletic pullover hoodie cardigans for Ben and Evelyn. However, he forgot cutleries, plates and cups. Fortunately, Aneida came well prepared. She brought two big outdoor picnic mats, potato salad, baked chicken, fried shrimps, and broccoli chicken casserole. She brought bottled water, napkins, cutleries, plates and cups. Aneida bought noise canceling headphones of different colors for Sheriff and Sarah. For Adam, she bought a Deluxe Executive Oakwood pen set in a wooden display case.

While Adam and all the children were casually dressed, Aneida wore an elegant blue long-sleeve floral applique maxi dress. She covered her hair with a blue foldable straw sun hat and wore designer sunglasses.

The picnic was quite enjoyable to all of them. After they had some things to eat, Ben and Sheriff went to play one-on-one basketball in the half court nearby. Evelyn and Sarah played scrabble for some time and later went for sightseeing in the park. It was as if the children knew when to leave Adam and Aneida alone on the picnic mat to chat about different things on the news and whatever else was on their minds.

Adam looked at Aneida and smiled.

"You look gorgeous," Adam remarked.

"Thank you very much," Aneida replied.

"I hope you brought a bugs spray," Adam inquired.

"Yes, because we are outdoors," Aneida explained.

"Great! So that we can send other bugs away and I will be the only one bugging you."

Aneida smiled.

The picnic significantly took Adams attention away from the marriage ceremony of Nora and Richard that was taking place at the same time in downtown Washington DC. Nora arrived at the banquet hall of Hotel Magnifica, which was a stone throw from the White House, in a horse drawn carriage while Richard arrived in a classic *Rolls Royce*. Nora emerged from her carriage in a stunning bridal dress which cost over seventy thousand dollars. The long sleeve white lace floral and crystal embellished gown with an astonishing hand-crafted embroidery in the center was complete with a six-feet length Chantilly lace train. Her white crystal-embellished shoes, the stylish hat with the Birdcage veil, gloves, and necklace all cost over thirty-five thousand dollars. It was certainly the most expensive outfit she has ever experienced. Richard was beaming with smiles in his black tuxedo with red cummerbund, bow tie and pocket square.

At exactly 1:45 pm, Adam picked his pen gift from Aneida while they were sitting alone on the picnic mat. He then took Aneida's left hand and drew a love symbol on the palm of her hand without removing the cover of the executive pen. This tickled Aneida and she giggled uncontrollably.

With a partially clear head that is devoid of Nora's image and a heart with little remnants of love for Nora, Adam felt that his heart was open to Aneida. He surmised that his head finally has a chance over his heart. Adam looked at Aneida adorably and called her in a soft voice.

"Aneida."

"Yes, Adam."

"Shall we begin writing a new chapter together in our book of lives?" Adam asked her with a smile. The question was clear. The intention was well understood. The meaning was obvious.

"Y-y-yes," Aneida stammered a heartfelt response fighting her tears.

At the same time, eleven miles away, Nora responded "I do!"

Part One: Section Three:
Who is staying married?

"Aaaaaaah! O my God!" Aneida exclaimed. Her shout was so loud that it shook the apartment. Ben and Evelyn rushed out of their rooms to the living room where they found their mum crying, clutching her chest with a card in her hand and was jumping up in excitement.

"Are you okay?" Ben asked being very worried.

"I am fine, Ben," Aneida replied.

"You scared us," Evelyn chimed in.

"I am so sorry. I did not mean to scare you," Aneida apologized.

At that point, Evelyn noticed the box on the table that was partially open. "What is that?" she asked.

"It is a box of gifts from Adam," Aneida responded.

"Your boyfriend? Are you guys dating or something?" Ben inquired.

"Is he going to be our step-dad?" Evelyn asked.

"Hmmm!" Aneida sighed and shrugged her shoulders.

It was obvious that Aneida was happy beyond description. Her children have not seen her this happy in a very long time. Aneida's head was in cloud nine. Sorry, cloud ninety. It was the first card Aneida had gotten since the Valentine Day card she got from Phillip the flop, her former husband just after their wedding eons ago.

The love transplant: The beginning of a new beginning

It was as if she just got a new pair of lungs
And can now inhale and exhale without difficulty
It was as if she just got a new heart
And love has started pumping out of her ventricles
It was as if she just got new kidneys
And can now eliminate toxic loneliness out of her system
It was as if she just got new corneas
And can now see clearly how beautiful love is
It was as if she just got a skin graft
And can now cover the burns she suffered from her failed
marriage.

Evelyn became too curious and tried to open the gift box on the table. Aneida slapped her hand lovingly and said, "leave my box alone!"

"Hmmm!" Evelyn grumbled. "Can I read the card?"

"Nope! It was not addressed to you."

"Hmmm!" Evelyn grumbled again.

"He sent something to both of you though," Aneida remarked as she started putting the card back into its envelope.

Ben turned back as he was already leaving to go back to his room to continue his video game.

"Great! What is it?" he asked with tempered expectation.

Aneida opened the gift box and handed Ben a book.

Ben was surprised at the gift and shouted "wow!" His mother gave him a copy of "*Becoming Kareem: Growing Up On and Off the Court,*" a book by the basketball legend Kareem Abdul-Jabbar. He was surprised at the gift because he had just casually mentioned to Sheriff before they went to play their one-on-one basketball challenge at the picnic that he loves basketball. He also stated that he would love to meet Kareem who is the player with the most points scored in the National Basketball Association (NBA) history.

"What about me?" Evelyn asked her mum.

"This is for you," she replied as she handed Evelyn a Designer Shoe Warehouse (DSW) $100 gift card with a note which reads: "On one condition: the high heel shoes should not make you taller than me!"

Evelyn was ecstatic. She did not realize that Adam heard her discussion with Sarah at the picnic. Sarah had mentioned how Aneida helped her with her shopping needs and that she also got high heel shoes. Evelyn had remarked that she wondered what it was like to wear high heels. Now she can get her own high heels for teenagers.

After she calmed down, she faced Aneida and asked, "what did he get you mum?"

"None of your business, Evelyn."

"C'mon mum!"

Aneida took out a gold gift box with a classic ribbon on top of it. It contained an assortment of chocolates.

"Mum, can I have a piece of chocolate?"

"Sure," Aneida replied and gave the box to Evelyn. Ben also helped himself to some chocolate pieces.

"Mum, your boyfriend pays a lot of attention," Evelyn commented with her mouth filled with chocolate.

"Well, what can I tell you? He is a doctor and they pay a lot of attention to details."

"Are you guys getting married soon?" Ben inquired as he reached for another piece of chocolate.

"Well…we will see how it goes," Aneida responded trying to be cautiously optimistic.

"I think he likes you though, but I like his daughter, Sarah. She is cute and nice," Evelyn opined.

Later, when she was alone in her room, Aneida opened a navy-blue velvet covered signature jewel box and took out a navy-blue luxurious pouch which contained a cable classics bracelet bangle with pearls and diamonds. She put it on her right wrist and admired how it looks on her. She then took the card and read it again beaming with smiles.

Getting to know you
The first time I saw you
I became dazed with the love for you
I breathe the same air as you
And I became breathless out of love for you
I ate the same food as you

And I had food poisoning of love for you
I drank the same drink as you
And I became intoxicated with love for you

The truth is very hard for me to handle
Passion is burning in my heart like a candle
A wonderful sensation that I never had before
A pleasurable feeling that I can never ignore

I really want to express it to you
I truly want to convey it to you
I am deeply in love with you

I love you

Nine months later, Adam looked out of the window of the *Airbus A320* to catch a glimpse of the setting sun. It was a glorious view. Then he turned his head to his side and smiled as he looked at the face of Aneida who was sleeping on the seat next to him. Evelyn and Sarah were also sleeping in the adjacent seats, but Sheriff and Ben were watching movies on the television sets in front of their seats. It had been an exciting trip, but now, they are all tired. Suddenly, Aneida opened her eyes because she heard the voice of the flight attendant who asked Adam his choice of the offered chicken and mushroom with mashed potato or cod fish with basmati rice. Aneida chose chicken while Adam chose the fish meal so that they can share both meals together as they have done in all flights that they have taken since leaving Washington Dulles airport to three European countries during these two weeks of honeymoon and family vacation combined trip.

Adam held Aneida's left hand and exposed her 18-karat yellow gold *Diamond Eternity* wedding band which encircled her ring finger. She smiled back at him. He lifted her hand and kiss the back of her hand.

"I love you," Adam whispered.

"I love you too honey," Aneida replied.

They have been married for three weeks. Of these, they have spent two weeks in Europe. They have visited Paris,

Vienna, and Frankfurt. They are now on their way back to Washington Dulles airport. Adam reflected on how happy he was to have been wrong about Aneida because of her age.

He recalled those annoying conversations he had with his friends in which Kamal, like the consistent Uncle Naysayer that he is, will always advise him to choose Aneida even though his heart was always with Nora. Now, Aneida has made him eat the proverbial crow even though she was totally unaware of it.

Nothing towers above Eiffel tower like love

Their first stop on the trip was the city of love itself, Paris. They booked three rooms. Ben and Sheriff shared a room. Evelyn and Sarah shared a room. Adam and Aneida kept each other warm. The experience they had in Paris was incredible for the whole week they spent in this beautiful city nicknamed "La Ville-Lumière" or the city of lights. The cuisine was great, but the potion sizes were smaller when compared to the sizes in the United States. The hotel suites were smaller in sizes too. For this newlywed, there was no controversy that Paris is the City of Lights and the City of Love. They saw the light in each other's eyes while love was overflowing from their hearts. In Paris, they visited the iconic Eiffel Tower, The Louvre, and Arc de Triomphe de l'Étoile.

You will feel good when you are triumphant

They visited the Palace of Versailles in the outskirts of Paris which was the royal residence of King Louis XIV. Fortunately, they did not plan anything else for that day as the tour of the magnificent palace and its garden became a full day of activities. They also spent a whole day for a trip to Normandy D-Day beaches to remember the heroes of World War II. Throughout their stay, in Paris and the outskirts, they enjoyed the food. Occasionally, the children craved American style cuisine. The only problem with the Paris trip was the Charles de Gaulle airport. The processing through the security line was very slow and laborious. There were lots of travelers on this day when they were leaving for Vienna. Fortunately, they made their two-hour flight just in the nick of time. After they arrived in Vienna, they checked into their hotel and rested for some time. Later in the evening, they attended Mozart concert at the Golden Hall. In the morning, they decided to rest and visit the historic Schönbrunn Palace in the early afternoon. On their way to the Palace, Ben noted that some places on the map of Vienna and stops on the underground train system ended in "Platz" such as Stephansplatz, Maria-Theresien-Platz and Heldenplatz. This made him remember somebody he adores in the United States.

"These places remind me of Ms Elaine Platz," Ben remarked.

"Who is she?" Sheriff asked.

"She is my counselor in school," Ben replied.

"Maybe her ancestors are from Vienna," Aneida suggested.

"I don't know, but I will surely ask her when we get back to school. She is a very nice and caring counselor. She is the one who advised me to take science courses. She thinks that I will be a good doctor," Ben related.

"Like Adam," Aneida commented while holding Adam's left hand while shooting him a lovely smile.

"Better than me," Adam responded smiling as he pat Ben on the shoulder.

How many people used to live in this Schonbrunn Palace with its 1,441 rooms? What was it like back when this palace was full of life?

They visited the imperial Schonbrunn Palace and marveled at the magnificence of the 1,441-room palace. It was the summer palace of the Habsburg monarchs. Unfortunately, they were not allowed to enter the rooms when they visited. They also visited the Schonbrunn Zoo before they left for Frankfurt in Germany. Quite boastfully in Vienna, people made them realize that the famous breakfast croissant delicacy was started by a Viennese while he was living in Paris.

They found Vienna to be a very interesting city and the underground train system was incredibly efficient and always on time.

The taxi ride from Frankfurt Airport to their hotel took about thirty minutes. The traffic was free flowing and was not comparable in anyway to leaving the District of Columbia National Reagan airport during rush hour.

Romerberg is an exciting public space in Frankfurt, Germany.

In Frankfurt, the family visited many places of interest. These include the Romerberg, Stadel Museum, Palmengarten and a number of fine diverse cuisine from different parts of the world. They had a fantastic dinner at a Turkish restaurant in Frankfurt am Main. However, the most memorable activity by Adam and Aneida was their joining the tradition of love locks on the Eiserner Steg love bridge to the admiration of their children.

Love locks on the bridge joining our hearts forever in Frankfurt, Germany.

Adam and Aneida shared and enjoyed the meal brought by the flight attendant. The chicken and mushroom with mashed potato was excellent and the cod fish with basmati rice was outstanding. No sooner did the flight attendant remove their food trays when the plane shook because of turbulence. The pilot put the 'fasten seatbelt' sign back on and informed the passengers of the turbulence. He urged them to remain seated with their seatbelts fastened. He then asked the flight attendants to suspend services and take their seats as he planned to increase the flight altitude to minimize the effect of the turbulence. Adam continued to hold Aneida's left hand adoringly. The announcement from the pilot had no meaning to him. His head, his mind and his body were in the clouds literally and figuratively. When the turbulence was over, Adam took out SkyVista, the in-flight magazine, from the back pouch of the seat in front of him and informed Aneida to read page eighty-five. She opened it and covered her mouth as tears of joy rolled down her cheeks from what she read. Apparently, when she was sleeping, Adam was looking at her and he wrote down his feelings in the empty space on page eighty-five of the SkyVista magazine.

A taste of love
A taste of love
Is what I get
Whenever I meet you

A feel of love
Is what sense
Whenever I am around you

A sight of love
Is what I observe
Whenever I see you

A smell of love
Is what I perceive
Whenever I am with you

A sound of love
Is what I hear
Whenever I touch you

A touch of love
Is what I feel
Whenever I hold you.

I love you Aneida.

49

Adam took a glance at the children. All of them were watching different movies on the television sets in front of their seats. Adam recalled when they were planning their modest wedding and were discussing the roles for the children. Even though they all appeared to be eager for the wedding to take place, they did not want to play any role at the event.

"C'mon guys! We are not asking you to be pall bearers," Adam expressed to them. "We are only asking you to be flower boys and girls."

"Dad, we are too old for that," Sheriff opined.

Adam looked at Aneida, but she just smiled and did not say anything.

"So, what do you guys want to do then?" Adam asked them.

"I will give mum away in marriage," Ben volunteered.

"What will her dad do then?" Adam asked him.

"Maybe both of us can give her away in marriage together. I will hold her right hand and he can hold her left hand."

"Okay with me so long as both of don't overstretch my wife's hands otherwise I will come and take her hands from both of you," Adam issued a stern warning which made all of them laugh.

"I will be your best man," Sheriff volunteered.

"Are you trying to run away with my wife too?" Adam asked his son chuckling.

"Sarah and I will be the bridesmaids," Evelyn suggested.

"Deal!" Aneida shouted.

"Is your wedding dress tail going to be long and too heavy for both of us to carry?" Sarah asked with genuine concern.

"Highly unlikely," Aneida responded with a reassuring tap on Sarah's left shoulder. "As a matter of fact, I will not be wearing a wedding dress with a tail."

Unlike the lavish marriage of Nora and Richard which featured a live band and a 5-tier cake that fed 150 elite guests, the marriage ceremony of Adam and Aneida was a private event that was only attended by the families of Adam and Aneida and a few of their friends. Kamal and Ray were also in attendance. They did not poke fun at Adam at the marriage ceremony. They did enough of that the week before the wedding when Kamal organized 'the most boring bachelor party ever' for Adam. Kamal had promised Adam that he would throw him a unique bachelor party after which everything will be exciting. The so-called party was only attended by Adam, Kamal and Ray. Kamal picked up Ray and Adam in his car that afternoon without telling Adam where the party was going to be held. Kamal had decided to show Adam what he would not be missing in raising little kids from Nora by organizing the so-called bachelor party at *Chuck E Cheese*. Jokingly, he told attendants at the venue that it was Adams birthday party for a new beginning. Even though they did not bring any kid to the entertainment center, they actually played a lot of the games in the arcade while poking fun at Adam. Later, they sat down for some discussions and ordered pizza.

"If you were getting married for the first time as a young man, I would have been giving you some marriage tips and advice by now," Kamal regretted.

"Still go ahead. An old dog can still learn new tricks," Adam encouraged him.

"Yes. An old dog can still get new ticks," Ray suggested.

"C'mon Ray, will you ever be serious?" Adam asked Ray.

"Of course. He will be serious when Desiree is shouting… Yes! Yes! Yes!" Kamal interjected.

"You guys are really crazy, absolutely crazy, totally crazy," Ray concluded.

Adam faced Kamal and said "let me guess. Your first advice will be for me to be spontaneous and show my affection for Aneida."

"Absolutely not!" Ray interrupted. "What has that gotten me?"

All the guys nodded in agreement.

"Honestly, my hope is for Aneida not be like you described Desiree."

"I agree brother, and I wish you well," Ray concurred.

"Per my marriage advice," Kamal started.

"Yes. I am listening with rapt attention," Adam responded.

"Even though I am talking to you, an old experienced bachelor…" Kamal paused.

"C'mon Kamal. Your preamble is killing me!" Adam exclaimed.

"But you have a lot of experience already," Kamal countered.

"I really want to hear what you have to say. So, let us assume that you are advising a young man in his twenties who is getting married for the first time. What will you say to him?"

Kamal cleared his throat and spoke with authority.

"**Number one:** See your marriage as a relationship between two imperfect people who need each other on their way to perfection. However, if one of you must take charge to make hard decisions, then it must be you as the husband. You are ultimately responsible for the kingdom. That said, you don't lose anything when you consult her even in those trying moments."

"**Number two:** Always manage your own finances even if your wife is the number one Certified Public Accountant (CPA) in the world or the Chair of the Board of Governors of the Federal Reserve System of the United States or the Chancellor of the Exchequer of the United Kingdom. It does not matter to me at all because in your kingdom, you must be in charge of your own finances. It has nothing to do with how prudent your wife is. It has everything to do with you being *the man*. This is because you have got to take care of the financial responsibilities no matter how much your wife makes. If your wife is a billionaire, never plan your life around her earnings. It will only rob you of your manhood, especially if that is important to you. Honestly, I expect it to be important to you."

"That is deep!" Adam exclaimed.

Ray nodded in agreement and remarked "I can only imagine what my situation will be if I needed money from Desiree."

Kamal continued with firmness in his voice.

"**Number three:** Take time for yourself. No matter how small. Have your man cave and your time to unwound. A good time is when you are in a gym or taking a walk by yourself. Remember, to give your wife her personal time too. Nonetheless, you need to have other things you do together other than dancing to the silent drums between the sheets."

"But ensure that you get adequate dancing between the sheets," Ray chimed in.

Kamal and Adam looked at Ray with prying eyes together.

"What!" Ray exclaimed. "I am just saying that...I mean...Well...It is really the most important part of the marriage. She may think that because she has the key to the gate of enjoyment, therefore, she is free to regulate it at will."

Kamal shook his head.

"Kamal, don't be bothered about Ray. The poor guy has been traumatized by Desiree so much that he is convinced that all women are like that," Adam commented.

"Really?" Ray questioned. "So, what percentage of men have had to endure 'No! Leave me alone' painful torment or suffered through the unjust, cruel and unusual punishment of 'I have a headache' from their wives when they desire a taste of human paradise?"

"I would say five percent," Kamal responded.

"Maybe ten percent....or.....up to fifteen percent," Adam opined.

"Try ninety percent," Ray affirmed with stern voice of authority.

"Really?" Adam expressed surprise.

"What do you think is at the center of the high divorce rate around us?" Ray pressed further.

"Really?" Adam expressed his surprise again.

> **Author's note:** For men: What percentage of husbands has put up with '*No! Leave me alone*' or '*I have a headache*' refusals from their wives?
>
> For women: What percentage of wives have said '*No! Leave me alone*' or '*I have a headache*' refusals to their husbands? Please indicate your gender when you respond.

Ray continued, "Yes. It is either the primary problem or a major contributing problem to most divorces. It is a revolving door of marriage misfortune. The guy doesn't get enough. The wife insists that she has given all he is going to get. The man outsources the difference on part-time basis and later becomes full-time. The wife accuses him of taking his treasures outside. The man is initially apologetic, then he becomes incalcitrant because his needs was never addressed to his satisfaction in the first place. The wife hides her treasures even more. The husband then says to her face, "bite me!" She gets angrier and bites him. He leaves. Soon afterwards, she regrets biting him."

"Well, I hope Aneida understands better than that," Adam expressed his hope.

"For your sake, I hope so too," Ray commented.

Kamal shook his head in agreement with Ray and then continued his advice.

"**Number four:** Discipline your children without punishing them. It is very important not to be punishing your children because your wife wanted you to do so. That will only make them afraid of you and resent you. Yet they will keep running to their mother not realizing that the punishment is coming from her by proxy. It is incredibly important that you should not punish your children for the errors of their mother. Although it may be very hard not to see your children as extensions of their mother who may be annoying the heck out of you, always try to be kind to your children. Adam, for you specifically, do not make your stepchildren feel like stepchildren."

"Hmmm!" Adam sighed.

Kamal paused.

"Is that all?" Ray asked Kamal.

"Nope! I have one more advice."

"Okay," Ray responded but Kamal did not speak. "So, what are you waiting for?" Ray raised his voice.

"My final advice is a tough one for everybody," Kamal regretted.

"And what would that be? Never get into an argument?" Adam suggested chuckling.

"Interestingly, you are close....but not quite correct."

"C'mon Kamal! Be out with it," Ray was beginning to lose patience.

"**Number five**: Practice the three rules of seventy," Kamal advised.

"What did you mean?" Adam inquired.

"You should count up to seventy before responding to an annoying statement. You should give your spouse seventy excuses for making a mistake. Finally, if you put up with your spouse for seventy years, things will definitely be better by then, guaranteed."

"That is funny," Adam chuckled.

"Which part?" Kamal asked him.

"By the time you put up with your spouse for seventy years....that is... if you are still alive, you will have no strength to fight him or her anymore," Adam explained.

"That is the whole idea," Kamal concurred. "Live together beyond death."

"I have one advice for you," Ray stated.

"I am all ears," Adam responded.

"Although it is very hard, but do not hold your responsibility as a hostage because you want to claim your right," Ray advised. "This is applicable to both the husband and the wife. In the end both of them will be pointing accusatory fingers at each other in the divorce court saying, 'it is your fault!' However, if they had both kept doing their responsibilities to each other, their communications will not break down completely, and they will easily resolve their differences."

"And there will be less business for those horrible divorce attorneys who are more like vultures on feeding frenzies on carcasses of dead marriages," Kamal expressed while remembering his divorce proceedings with Kandie.

"Wow! You really have negative opinions about divorce attorneys," Ray concluded. "They are merely doing their best representing their clients. The onus is on the couples not to find themselves in that situation."

"Yes. I agree with you. They should not let their marriages die and become carcasses for vultures in the garb of divorce attorneys or maybe we should consider divorce attorneys as grave diggers who would rather bury marriages for their selfish interests," Kamal emphasized.

"Okay guys! Don't fight for free," Adam chimed in while trying to reduce the verbal tension building up between Kamal and Ray. "If you guys want to fight, let us get Bob Arum or Don King involved. I will be the manager for both of you. I have my money on upper cuts and power punches, and I support the winner."

"You are crazier than I thought," Kamal responded shaking his head.

After spending about two hours in *Chuck E Cheese*, the unusual bachelor party came to an end and Kamal dropped his friends off.

"Thank you very much for organizing the best bachelor party in the history of the world," Adam remarked to Kamal as he was exiting Kamal's car.

"My pleasure. I am all in for any intervention that will prevent a premature heart attack for my friend," Kamal responded with a veiled approval of Aneida's candidacy as the better choice for Adam rather than Nora.

Adam's mind returned to the present as he continued to rub Aneida's let hand like an amateur massage therapist. He was happy that things have turned out well for him and Aneida. After another two hours of flight, the voice of the pilot came on air informing the passengers that they have started their descent towards Washington Dulles Airport and that passengers should return to their seats and fasten their seatbelts. Soon afterwards, they picked their car at the economy parking lot at the airport and drove home. Adam parked in the driveway. They exited the car and started packing their bags into the house. The children carried their bags, their gift items, and souvenirs they bought from their vacation. Adam looked at Aneida as she was walking into the house pulling her carry-on roller bag. Her flowing flowery pattern maxi gown with hibiscus embroidery was dancing to the sounds of the breeze. She looked stunning.

"Although Nora would have been a lot more fun, but those who say, 'life begins at forty' do have a point." Adam said to himself as he admired the grace with which Aneida walks. "I guess at that age you begin to combine grace with maturity, and it does not mean your beauty has faded like old jeans."

About two months later, Nora was feeling quite lonely in the exquisite apartment she once shared with Richard who has now left her and moved back to New York. She decided to visit her parents. Although she has always talked to her parents over the phone, she has not seen them in three months. After a few minutes in the living room, she decided to go to her former room upstairs. She had a nostalgia. Nora quickly realized that she does not belong there anymore even though she left less than a year previously. She looked at her old room. Although it felt familiar, but it now has the stench of failure. The ghost of unfulfilled dreams flies through the walls. She saw a copy of *Essence* magazine on the floor of the closet. It looked familiar. It must have fallen when she was hurriedly packing her stuff just after her wedding. She had given away a lot of her stuff. She opened the magazine and found a familiar card. This was the last card she got from Adam. It was his expression of his love for her after the awkward family dinner which was complicated by the discovery that Adam and Nora's mum, were adversaries in middle school. A part of Nora felt happy to have found this card because it now became the only memento she has of Adam's love for her. Although Adam had sent her many cards in the past couple of years, she had destroyed all of them just after her engagement to Richard. Tears welled up in Nora's eyes. The card felt special to her in a weird way. It was just fortuitous that she still had the card. She had thrown it on her desk after reading it and it must have accidentally been tucked in this magazine. She opened the card and read it.

Over and over, again and again
When I spoke to you
That I truly love you
I wasn't lying to you
I was being truthful

When I told you
That I need you
I wasn't teasing you
I was being forthright

When I informed you
That I want you
I wasn't deceiving you
I was being sincere

When I revealed to you
That I desire you
I wasn't cajoling you
I was being honest

When I indicated to you
That I yearn for you
I wasn't deluding you
I was being genuine

When I disclosed to you
That I long for you
I wasn't joking with you
I was being candid

When I conveyed to you
That I hanker after you
I wasn't hoodwinking you
I was being precise

When I talked to you
That I am attracted to you
I wasn't misleading you
I was being faithful

When I briefed you
That I am craving you
I wasn't swindling you
I was being real

When I communicated to you
That I have feelings for you
I wasn't misinforming you
I was being plainspoken

When I enlightened you
That I want to be with you
I wasn't misguiding you
I was being accurate

When I declared to you
That my ideal partner is you
I wasn't flattering you
I was being frank

When I apprised you
That I care about you
I wasn't tricking you
I was being straightforward

When I expressed to you
That I am passionate about you
I wasn't entrapping you
I was being blunt

When I uttered to you
That I am very fond of you
I wasn't bamboozling you
I was being explicit

When I notified you
That I don't want to live without you
I wasn't seducing you
I was being factual

I hope that my message is very clear that
I really love you
I want to be with you
I don't want to be without you
I really love and care about you

I love you

Nora was moved to tears but quickly dry them. It was too late. Unfortunately, anybody can rewind a clock, but nobody can rewind time. Nora remembered how Adam used to look at her, it was very obvious that he truly loved her. Now, what Adam had told her made sense. Adam had opined that, "the only thing heart that you will get from this spoiled brat is a heartburn if you are lucky, otherwise it is only going to be a painful heart attack." At that time, she felt Adam said that because he wanted to convince her that he was a better candidate for her. In hindsight, even though he wanted to marry her, it was now painfully obvious that Adam was also trying to warn her.

She sighed as it dawned on her that she chose to marry Richard. Unfortunately, he has now left her after only eleven months of marriage. All she has to show for her marriage to Richard is her protuberant abdomen. Her only companion is her seven-month-old pregnancy. Nora vowed never to let what happened to her happen to her baby. She regretted being influenced by her mum and not encouraged to follow her heart. Nora wished that her dad did not sit on the fence but had advocated more for her. It was not his fault though. She never told him that she would have preferred to be married to Adam despite the age difference and the presence of other children from his deceased wife.

Nora felt wiser. "It never works," she said to herself. "When a parent of a wayward son assumes that if he gets married to a decent girl, he will settle down and become better, they are just putting somebody else's daughter in a precarious situation. If the parents of the girl know this, why would they give their daughter away to such a guy no matter how rich his family is?" Nora wondered. "They would have just failed their daughter like what happened to me because the conqueror mentality that these people have never goes away until they suffer a major calamity. It is the other people that should avoid being subservient to these folks."

Nora felt bitter that her marriage to Richard was an example of such failed rehabilitation experiments. Unfortunately, her mother bought into it and ruined her own daughter in the process. She started criticizing her father again. She felt that he should have stepped in a little more to rescue her from her mum's terrible decision. Again, she gave him a slack. It was not really his fault. His father asked her, but she was the one that did not open up to him completely about her feelings. Afterall, her dad was the one who put his foot down against all oppositions from her mum for them to invite Adam to meet her family in the first place. Although it turned out to be a disaster because her mum would not give Adam a chance due to a grudge which she has been harboring for three decades. Notwithstanding, if she could go back in time, she would discuss a lot more with her dad. After all, he is a man and men should be able to understand and evaluate men better.

Tears started rolling down the cheeks of Nora again as the feelings of betrayal filled up her heart against her mum. She started blaming her mum again for getting her married to Richard. She felt that her mum just wanted to live her fantasy dream in high society through her daughter. Even if it was sincere that she simply wanted a better life for her daughter by trying to get her what she felt that she did not have, it was doubtful if she really considered what her daughter may really want. Unfortunately, it is now painfully obvious that the most important thing her mother had is what her daughter is now lacking - a loving and caring husband.

The irony of it all was that her mother never felt welcomed in the so called 'high society' she craved. All she realized was that she was dealing with a class of people who look down on others and have the "we are the conquerors" mentality. The only common interest they have is about making money. This is the only thing that makes them come together in their cut-throat competitive world. Nora recalled being appalled in a social function she had attended with Richard soon after their wedding. In the party, people were busy gossiping about a close friend of theirs who also happened to be a business associate of theirs. Yet, when somebody remarked 'he is not really rich. He is just a single digit millionaire,' they all laughed. This had made Nora feel totally out of place.

"Character and not wealth should be the basis of choosing

a spouse," Nora said to herself while drying her tears as she closed the door of her former room. She still wished that she could somehow turn back the hand of time. However, she must keep moving forward without Richard. That is the only thing that matters. Nothing else matters now. She must stay strong for her unborn child.

Part Two

Decisive Decision:
The story of Kamal

Part Two: Section One:
Who is being protected?

After multiple visits to the fertility clinic and a somewhat unending barrage of laboratory and imaging tests, Bonita was ready for the next phase of her fecundity enhancing program.

"Under normal circumstances, a woman only produces an egg once a month," Dr Childlove commented.

"This is a circumstance in which I actually wish we produce eggs like birds to increase the chances of having a baby," Bonita voiced her wishes. Kamal put his right hand on Bonita's left hand to reassure her that everything will be fine.

"Well, the chances of human beings are pretty good and definitely higher than emperor penguins who lay only one egg per year," Dr Childlove commented trying to give some soothing hope to Kamal and Bonita.

"I prefer the chances of hens. They lay eggs almost everyday, with an average of five eggs per week," Bonita reaffirmed.

"I get your point. However, the biology of humans does not function that way. What we can attempt is to increase how many eggs you produce in a cycle to increase the chances of fertilization," Dr Childlove suggested.

Bonita looked at Kamal and they both smiled and nodded in agreement.

The calendar in the bedroom developed multiple colored markings on it indicating different stages of Bonita's cycle. It was a crazy obsession in every way imaginable. There were many things to do of which counting days is the easiest. There was the temperature monitoring, the ovulation signs evaluation, and the targeted and near regimented intimacy without intimate moments. The most challenging part was when the unwanted monthly guest shows up to Bonita in form of a period that she would rather not have. Bonita will become profoundly dejected until the couple is ready to try again.

After five months of failures, Bonita did not see her period in the sixth month of taking fertility pills. The couple were elated but afraid at the same time. They debated how long they should wait before getting a pregnancy test done. Her period has always been regular, but she had not seen it for three days. The couple were cautiously optimistic that she was three days pregnant.

"Do you feel anything?" Kamal asked Bonita.

"No! I don't think that I should be able to feel the baby move at this time," Bonita responded.

"That is not what I meant. I mean….er….er….when women are pregnant…things do happen….you know," Kamal struggled with his words.

"You mean like me craving …or something …you know…like me saying that you should get me some cupcakes and ice cream from *Dairy King* on Georgia Avenue?"

"Are you trying to get me… to get you… cupcakes and ice cream?" Kamal sought clarification while pointing at himself and Bonita while saying.. 'get me.. to get you.'

Bonita smiled in appreciation. "I am only pulling your legs darling. You look so nervous. I have only missed my period for three days."

"Well, I just wanted to know that you are okay," Kamal replied.

"If what you were wondering is whether I was feeling nauseous…."

"Exactly!" Kamal interjected.

Bonita shook her head and beckoned her husband to

come to her. She then took Kamal's right hand and hugged him. "Thank you very much for your care darling. I am fine."

Two days later, Bonita still has not seen her period. The pregnancy anxiety increased astronomically. Kamal decided to go to the nearby CVS Pharmacy store and bought an Error Proof Pregnancy Test kit. When he got home, Bonita was no longer in the living room where he had asked her to wait and relax for him to go and get the pregnancy test kit.

"Honey! Honey! Where are you?" Kamal raised his voice trying to find Bonita.

Then he thought he heard a soft sob in the bathroom. Kamal went closer and heard Bonita trying desperately to control her cries. Kamal opened the door and found Bonita hunched over on the bathroom countertop with wash hand basin trying to dry her tears with the facial napkin. Her eyes were sad and red with tears. Kamal gently put the pregnancy test kit on the countertop and placed his hand gently on Bonita's left shoulder.

"What happened?" He asked her.

"I came to the bathroom to obtain a urine sample for the pregnancy test only for me to notice that my period has come," Bonita explained, and her weeping got louder.

Kamal became very sad, not because of the dashed hope of pregnancy, but because Bonita was very sad. He gently pulled Bonita from the countertop and hugged her whispering into her ears in a calming reassuring tone "everything will be fine."

I believe in us
The wind may appear to be at a standstill
The stars may appear to have lost their twinkle
The diamond may appear to have lost its sparkle
The sun may appear to have lost its sunshine
The moon may appear to have lost its cool reflections
The river may appear to have stopped flowing
The breeze may appear to have stopped blowing
The ocean may appear to be stagnant
The clown may appear to be frowning

The bulldog may appear to be toothless
The dog may appear to be hoarse
The parrot may appear to be silent

My darling, we will pull through
My dear, we will beat this
My wife, we will succeed
My love, we will persevere
Baby, we have each other
And we will endure together

Three months later, Kamal and Bonita completed their initial evaluations and settled their initial bills for the in vitro fertilization process. Their anxiety and financial hit have now gone through the roof, but a healthy baby is worth the world in their minds. The initial price tag was fifteen thousand dollars ($15,000) for the in vitro fertilization procedure without medications. All the bills were paid out of pocket. The process included egg recovery for which she had to take mega doses of hormones to dramatically increase egg production. The doctor started with seven fertilized eggs and left them growing for about seven days. She got injected with hormones for seven days to make her body feel as if she was already in a pregnant state prior to the implantation. The implantation is not like digging the soil to plant flowers, trees or shrubs, it was merely a five minutes procedure of injecting the embryos into the womb.

Bonita was given a mandatory bed rest for three days during which she couldn't sleep out of anxiety. She felt as if she was walking in the shadows of the unknown. It really broke Kamal's heart to watch his loving wife go through this harrowing experience in order to have a baby. The experience was particularly traumatic for Kamal because he could not really help her except with kind words and general warm presence. It was a period of total inward reflection for Kamal to even think that a child can grow up to be disrespectful to his or her parents. He felt that there is no justifiable circumstance that a child should even show discontent to his or her parent, let alone to outrightly disrespect them. He was convinced that it is impossible for a child to ever repay his or her parents, no matter what they become in the future. Even though Kandie did not want to be pregnant when she got pregnant with Kamal junior, she did not encounter any hardship at all. He remembered that he had sabotaged the condom to get Kandie pregnant when they were married because he wanted them to have a family complete with children when Kandie was wasting time and was not getting her priorities right. A part of him still regretted sabotaging the condom as it was the major problem that led to the end of his marriage with Kandie. Unfortunately, their relationship ended due to excessive reaction and lack of forgiveness from Kandie even though he had confessed his error willingly.

"Well, that was an unpleasant history," Kamal said to himself and shook his head as if to shake the bad memory away from his head.

Kamal took two weeks of his annual vacation to coincide with the time of the implantation so that he was at home with Bonita at all times. Kamal ensured that he provided Bonita with all her needs and did not let her do anything strenuous in order for her to adhere strictly to the recommended bed rest.

Bonita felt she was treated like a queen that she is, at least, in the Brown's kingdom. Sometimes, she feels that Kamal may be overdoing it 'a little bit' especially in the early phases.

"Where are you going baby," Kamal asked Bonita.

"I am going to the bathroom," Bonita responded.

"But the doctor said that you should be on bed rest," Kamal reminded her.

"Yes. I am on bed rest," Bonita reassured him.

"But you just said that you are going to the bathroom just now," Kamal reiterated.

"C'mon! baby. I can go to the bathroom while on bed rest," Bonita explained.

"I was thinking of getting you breakfast, lunch and dinner in bed. I will give you bed bath myself and I will be going to the store shortly to get you some adult diapers. That way you have no need to leave the bed."

"I really appreciate it darling, but I am fine," Bonita reassured him.

The fact was that Kamal did bring breakfast, lunch and dinner to Bonita in the bedroom. Many a time, they will eat together in the bedroom. Sometimes, they will go to the dining table together after much persuasion from Bonita.

Ten days later, Bonita's pregnancy test was positive. About ten weeks later her sonogram revealed two beating hearts in her womb. Two of the fertilized eggs implanted. Kamal and Bonita were expecting twins. They were elated.

About three months later, Kamal accompanied Bonita to see Dr Childlove as he has always done during her obstetrics visit. That morning, Dr Childlove performed a sonogram to assess the babies. The sonogram was normal. The babies were developing well. Bonita even mentioned that she was beginning to feel the babies move. Dr childlove had joked that it seemed the babies were playing 'touch football' which made Kamal remarked that given their Hispanic genes, they were probably playing soccer instead. Bonita disagreed with her husband and the doctor by claiming that the babies were swimming. She then promised to guide them to become Olympic gold medalists in swimming in the future.

When they got home after the doctor's visit, Kamal decided to get an oil change and tire rotation at the car dealership and run some errands while Bonita decided to take a nap and then cook an early dinner for them. At that point Bonita had taken an extended leave of absence without pay from her job in order to decrease her stress and optimize their chances of a successful pregnancy outcome.

Bonita suddenly developed some pains in her lower abdomen when she was in the kitchen. She stopped cooking and went to lay down in the bedroom. When the pain did not abate, she took two tablets of acetaminophen and called Kamal who left the store immediately driving on the beltway I-495 like a mad man. By the time he got home thirty minutes and three speeding camera photographs later, Bonita was having excruciating pain and had started bleeding profusely requiring her to use sanitary towels.

Kamal called 911 immediately.

At the same time thirty miles away, Kandie was also thinking about Kamal albeit for a different reason. Kandie felt that Kamal has betrayed his true self by wearing the Giorgio Armani suit without thanking her for the gift. She felt betrayed. However, she quickly blamed it on Bonita, 'the husband-snatching Mexican' as she refers to her out of contempt. "This woman has been preventing my son from seeing his father regularly and thereby, blocking me from reconnecting with my husband," Kandie opined in anger. Kandie complemented herself for her extreme patience in talking herself out of doing something drastic about it while hoping that Kamal will come to his senses. However, that hope is now seemingly a long-drawn-out process and she genuinely felt she needed to give the process a nudge.

Kandie took out her laptop and visited the Department of Homeland and Sea Security web page as she has done multiple times since she received those heart-breaking photos of 'stupid' romance between Kamal and Bonita. There was no doubt in Kandie's mind that Bonita wanted to mock her, otherwise there was absolutely no reason for her to have sent her those nonsensical pictures especially saying that she was giving Kamal all her love. She looked at her cellphone screen which cracked when she accidentally dropped it after she got those annoying pictures from Bonita. The cracked cellphone screen gave Kandie all the motivation she needed.

Part Two: Section Two:
Who is the protector?

Bonita was rushed to the hospital by emergency medical services and was immediately transferred to the obstetrics and gynecology department. Fortuitously, Dr Childlove was physically in the hospital when Kamal called his office to notify him. Therefore, he was on hand when Bonita arrived in an ambulance to the hospital.

Dr Childlove and the nursing staff received Bonita and attended to her immediately while Kamal was asked to wait in the waiting area adjacent to the labor ward. Kamal could not sit down. He was sweating boulders and his heart was racing like the automobiles at the Indianapolis Motor Speedway for Indy 500 competition. Kamal was pacing up and down while his brain drew a blank. He later sat down resting his head on his hands.

After a grueling one hour and thirty minutes that felt like eternity, Dr Childlove walked into the waiting area with a gloomy look on his face. Kamal already knew that something major has happened.

"How is my wife?" Kamal asked Dr Childlove with a lot of anxiety in his voice as he quickly rose to his feet.

Dr Childlove shook his head. Sadness was written all over his face in bold letters. With a broken voice, he replied "Your wife is fine Mr Brown, but I am afraid…"

"Can I see her?" Kamal asked Dr Childlove interrupting him. It was as if he already knew the bad news or he simply cared more about his loving wife's health.

"Yes. You may see her. Unfortunately...I.. I ..I am so sorry sir...b-b-but the babies did not make it."

Bitter tears rolled down the eyes of Kamal as he was led to the room where Bonita was partially asleep from the effect of the medications that she was given. She opened her eyes and tried to force a smile on seeing her husband. However, she noted his tear-laden eyes and she started crying again. Kamal sat on a chair next to Bonita's bed and held her left hand tightly. Then, he kissed the back of her hand and tried to force a smile.

"I am glad to see that you are okay," Kamal remarked.

"But our babies are not!" Bonita commented and busted into tears.

Kamal could no longer control himself and he started weeping too. Dr Childlove stood speechless. He let out a sigh of sorrow subconsciously while the Charge Nurse who had entered the room to console them could not help crying too. She took some facial napkins to dry her tears as she muffled "our thoughts and prayers are with you and your family in these challenging moments."

"Thank you very much. We really appreciate your efforts and care," Kamal replied.

It was a painful loss. Mother love could not make them stay in the womb for any additional length of time. Father love was just not enough to keep them alive. Modern medicine could not prevent the departure of the souls of these unborn precious twins. It was a loss of two family members in one day. It was even more devastating that they had a sonogram done that morning and the babies were fine. Kamal and Bonita had sacrificed a lot in money, energy and time in order to increase their chances of having children. They had avoided anything that could remotely cause any problem including 'terrific touchy tango' between the sheets. Bonita had used all her annual vacations, her sick leave and has now started an extended leave of absence without pay. Unfortunately, it was not meant to be.

After hospitalization for two days, Bonita was discharged from the hospital. The day after she arrived at home, Kamal had to run some errands, so he left Bonita on the sofa as she slept in the living room. Suddenly, there was a loud knock on the door. When there was no response, the intensity of the knock at the door increased.

"Police! Open up!" The voice at the door commanded.

Bonita struggled to get to her feet wondering what was going on. She felt a bit dizzy when she stood up too quickly but regained her balance after holding on to the edge of the sofa.

"I will be right there! She shouted on top of her lungs as much as she could."

After a few seconds, the voice at the door repeated the command.

Bonita managed to get to the door and opened it. She found a man and a woman in civilian clothes wearing point blank body armor with the police insignia written on it.

"Good afternoon officers. How may I help you?" Bonita addressed the police officers.

"I am Detective Larry and this is Detective Abacay. We are from the Immigration and Custom Enforcement of the Department of Homeland and Sea Security. We just have a few questions for you mam. May we come in?"

"Yes, please," Bonita obliged and showed them into the living room. She sat on the sofa. "I am so sorry, but I am weak. I was just discharged from the hospital. Can I get you something? Water? Tea? Juice?"

"No. Thank you mam," Detective Larry responded.

Both detectives then gave Bonita a copy of their business cards identifying them as field agents for Immigration and Custom Enforcement section of the Department of Homeland and Sea Security.

"May we see your international passport mam?" Detective Larry asked.

"I am sorry. I am not sure exactly where it is, but I am pretty certain that it has probably expired by now. I have not travelled outside the country in years. May I know why you want to see my passport though?" Bonita responded as she got up to go and look for her passport in the bedroom.

"We are investigating a tip that we got that you have overstayed your visa in the United States," Detective Larry explained.

"There must have been a misunderstanding of some sort. I didn't come to the United States with a visa," Bonita asserted looking puzzled at the allegation.

"What did you mean?" Detective Abacay chimed in.

"I was born in the United States….in El Paso, Texas to be precise. My parents are the ones who were immigrants from Mexico," Bonita affirmed.

"Really?" Detective Larry and Detective Abacay asked in unison.

"Yes. I was born in the University of El-Paso Medical Center," Bonita responded to the detectives as she started walking into the bedroom to look for her international passport.

Fortunately, she found it in her document box along with her birth certificate and brought them to the officers. Indeed, the passport expired about nine months previously. Detective Larry took the passport and the birth certificate and examined them carefully.

"They are legit," Detective Larry commented. He then gave the documents to Detective Abacay who also examined them. She then took pictures of the birth certificate and the international passport.

"Thank you very much mam. Have a nice day," Detective Abacay said to Bonita as she handed her back her birth certificate and her expired international passport.

"Thank you," Bonita replied.

Both officers then left the house.

Bonita stood motionless for a few seconds wondering about what had just transpired.

"Why would Immigration and Customs Enforcement agents come to her house? To deport her? Who gave them this false tip?" Bonita continued to ask herself many questions without answers. She felt a bit weak again and went to lay down again on the sofa wondering whether to call Kamal or just wait for him to get back home. She reflected on the conversation she had with the officers and suddenly, it dawned on her. Somebody gave a tip to Immigration and Custom Enforcement with the idea that she is an undocumented immigrant so that she can be deported from the United States. She immediately thought of her parents in El-Paso and called her father.

"Papa. Hola. Como estas," Bonita greeted her dad and asked about how he is doing.

"Muy bien gracias," her father replied that he is doing fine, and he inquired about Bonita's health and offered her words of encouragement following the loss of her pregnancy. He also inquired about Kamal and asked Bonita to extend his greetings to her husband.

Bonita then inquired about her mum and her father replied that they are fine. He then mentioned that two police officers just left their house. They were Immigration and Custom Enforcement officers and they came to verify their immigration status. He informed Bonita that they showed them their naturalization certificates which they obtain two months previously. They have been permanent residents of the United States for seven years prior to becoming citizens.

After Bonita exchanged pleasantries and reassurances with her father, she spoke with her mother who also comforted and prayed for her. She then hung up the phone.

Bonita was livid. "Who could be trying to deport me and my family from the United States?" She asked herself again. As if in a flash, she thought of Kandie. Bonita dismissed the idea immediately and said to herself, "even evil Kandie would not descend so low." However, a faint voice in her head remarked, "but you never know."

Bonita shook her head in amazement. Whoever was trying to deport her obviously did not know that she was born in the United States. The person did not realize that whenever she says that "My family is from Mexico," which she does very often, she was referring to her ancestral origin and that she is proud of her Hispanic heritage.

No doubt, whoever was 'this poisonous snake' did not realize that she started working immediately after she left high school so that she can raise enough money to support her family and to file for them to have legal stay in the United States. That was why she had a full-time job and a part-time job for many years in order to raise the money her family needed for their upkeep and their legal fees for their immigration processes. It was after those important things were taken care of that she decided to enroll in the University of Seattle to obtain her bachelor's degree as a mature student while still holding a full-time job in the hotel."

"Whoever was this snake, I hope he or she gets what he or she deserves," Bonita remarked as she fell asleep on the sofa.

When Kamal returned, he came home with takeout food order from *Hibachi grill*. The sumptuous meal consisted of sushi, chicken, tofu and salmon with fried rice and shrimp egg roll for him and Bonita. Over dinner, Bonita informed Kamal what happened when he was away. She mentioned the visit by the Immigration and Customs Enforcement agents to her and her parents simultaneously.

Kamal felt that it was suspicious. He was convinced that somebody must have sent them a false tip. However, he did not want to speculate who did so. Kamal held Bonita's hands lovingly while looking at her eyes that were beginning to well-up with tears and remarked, "we will be fine. These are just temporary challenges."

Two words
Lovely lady
Lively lover
Finest flower
Terrific treat
Vibrant view
Beautiful babe
Delightful darling
Desirable damsel
Gorgeous girl
Spectacular single
Sensational sweetheart
Pleasant partner

Fantastic friend
Comforting companion
Convivial colleague
Fantabulous fellow
Amazing associate
Magnificent mate

And my favorite two words to describe you now is:
Wonderful wife

But the favorite two words I will soon use to describe you is
Marvelous mother

"I love you Bonita. Always have, always will."

Part Two: Section Three:
Who lost protection?

The traumatic experience of the journey towards motherhood shook Bonita. She was very sad. She analyzed how much sacrifice she and her husband have made. A lot of time and money has been spent. Her health was also on the line when she needed to be rushed to the hospital in an ambulance. Unfortunately, at the end of the day, there is no baby to show for all the efforts and sacrifices made. This was particularly devastating for Bonita. Kamal tried to comfort her by reassuring her that all will be fine, but Bonita could not get her mind off the traumatic experience she had.

On a Saturday morning, about two weeks later, Kamal rested his head on Bonita's laps while she was sitting on the sofa in the living room. The television was on a sports channel in which some sports journalists and commentators were analyzing the upcoming game.

"We have been through a lot together and we can weather the storm together," Kamal explained.

"Can we consider adoption?" Bonita inquired.

"What?" Kamal exclaimed. "No way! We are not adopting anybody, and he lifted his head from her laps."

Kamal stood up pulling Bonita to her feet. He embraced her and she started crying on his shoulder. Kamal tapped her gently on her back and told her that adoption is not an option.

"But we can do a closed adoption or an open adoption…" Bonita tried to explain.

"Nope!" Kamal interjected.

"You know in open adoption, we can be involved with the people we are adopting from so that they know us and we know them. However, if we don't want them to engage with us, we can try closed adoption." Bonita explained further.

"Honey, we don't need to adopt anybody. What is the point? Will it be for us to pretend to the people that we have our own child? If the people we are trying to impress don't know, at least we will know that the child is not ours, right? So, what is the point?"

"Hmmm!" Bonita sighed.

Kamal continued, "and if the point is to assist another family in raising their child, then there is no point in adopting the child. We can still offer the same assistance without changing the child's name. There will be no need for the child to bear our name and give a false impression that the child belongs to us."

"Hmmm!" Bonita sighed again.

The best days are ahead
When the journey is long
When the obstacles are many
When the resources are limited
When the reward is not immediate

It becomes difficult not to be tired
It becomes challenging to stay focused
It becomes tough to keep going
It becomes hard not to give up

However, after every hardship comes relief
Verily, after every hardship comes relief
Therefore, let us keep up hope together
For happy endings are around the corner.

I love you
Forever more

I love you
For you deserve it
I love you
For you are my soulmate

Kamal kissed Bonita and remarked "Darling, our babies are already on the way. They took Echo airlines but their flight was delayed."

This reference to Echo airline made Bonita smile. She remembered that the rescheduling of Kamal's flight to Hawaii by Echo airline in Seattle Airport was the primary event that brought them together. Kamal had come with a complimentary voucher for lodging at the hotel where Bonita worked as a receptionist.

"That delay you had in Seattle was fortuitous for us," Bonita recalled with smile.

"This delay is going to be fortuitous for us too," Kamal commented. He then put his hand on Bonita's abdomen and remarked "I think our babies are boarding now!"

Bonita started laughing uncontrollably.

My sweet wonderful butterfly
Cute, brightly colored and beautiful
Rhythmic flying and purposeful
Sweet, easy going and joyful
Cool, never threatening and graceful
Knows directions clearly and dutiful
Nice, pleasant and resourceful
Purple, blue, orange, yellow and so colorful
You, me, and our children on the way, so fruitful.

About six week later, Bonita returned to Dr Childlove's office accompanied by Kamal. All of them tried to keep a positive attitude regarding the loss of the twin pregnancy.

"You know,.." Dr Childlove broke the ice.. "although we would have preferred a completely positive outcome, but the truth is that you got pregnant on the first try of in-vitro fertilization."

Bonita nodded in agreement.

"That is actually a very good sign," Dr Childlove concluded.

"Really?" Kamal asked.

"Yes. The average number of attempts before a successful pregnancy is three times and for some couples, the chances get better and peaks at about sixty percent after six attempts. Only one in three couples get pregnant after three in-vitro fertilization attempts. So, your odds are pretty good."

Kamal and Bonita held each other's hands in happy solidarity.

"The only issue is the cost associated with having to repeat the cycle of in-vitro fertilization," Dr Childlove explained.

"Hmmm!" Bonita sighed.

"No problem Doc, we will work it out and find a way," Kamal reassured Dr Childlove while he put a comforting hand on Bonita's left shoulder. At that moment, Kamal's phone rang. He looked at it and realized that the call was from Kandie. Kamal did not say a word, but he let the call go into his voice mail. At the conclusion of the clinic visit, they all agreed to meet again in two months to begin the planning for the second cycle of in-vitro fertilization.

When they reached home, Kamal listened to the message that Kandie left for him. The message simply stated "Hi Kamal. I know that you got the Giorgio Armani suit that I sent you even though you neither acknowledged it nor show any appreciation for my kind gesture. You have not even called or stopped by to check on your only child. Do you still want to continue to see him? Please give me a call when you get this message."

Kamal felt disgusted with Kandie's voicemail. It was so callous and so incredibly irritating. However, Bonita was sitting next to him on the sofa when he listened to the message. Therefore, he tried his best to mute his response. However, Bonita noticed that Kamal was unhappy with the message he got.

"Are you okay? Is everything alright?" Bonita asked Kamal.

"It is okay," Kamal responded trying to hide his anger. He felt that Kandie was threatening him regarding his son, but he decided to be patient. He definitely would not want to do anything that would upset Bonita, his wonderful wife. No doubt, he will need to address the problem from Kandie but taking care of Bonita is a lot more important.

Later in the evening, when Kamal and Bonita were having dinner, Kandie called again. Kamal summoned the last vestige of patience he had and did not pick the call again because he did not want Kandie to make him angry. This time around, Kandie did not leave a message. Rather she called back again and again in close successions. Kamal thought of blocking Kandie's number albeit temporarily, but he decided against it and decided to just be patient.

After six unanswered calls, Kandie sent Kamal a text message which simply read: "Kamal, pick up the phone. I know that you are screening my call." Kamal read the text message but rather than replying her, Kamal put his phone in silent mode and continued to eat his dinner. Bonita was sure that something was going on with the caller who was persistent in calling Kamal. It was too obvious that Kamal did not want to engage the person. This gave Bonita a pause. Her mind wondered if Kamal was just avoiding the caller so that she will not know what was going on. "Who was the caller?" Bonita asked herself. Suddenly, her mind added one and two together and she got twelve million. "Is Kamal having an affair? Should she try and look at his phone to figure out what is going on?" The thoughts sent shivers down her spine. She wanted to ask him about the caller, but the rational part of her mind advised against spying on her husband. It reassured her to trust her husband's judgement. Bonita chuckled and Kamal noticed. He smiled at her, but he did not say anything. They continued their dinner.

"The food was so outstanding, I almost ate the plates," Kamal commented when they finished eating. Bonita started clearing the plates off the dining table.

"Thank you," Bonita replied smiling.

Later, when they retired to bed, Kamal held Bonita's right hand and commented, "I hope Kandie has not been bothering you."

"Not anymore," Bonita replied. "Has she been bothering you?"

"She has been getting on my nerves," Kamal responded.

"She is a pain in the neck, in the chest, in the leg, in the rear….in fact, she is a pain everywhere. Unfortunately, she is a pain you can't treat with any medication."

"Hmmm!" Bonita sighed. She has now realized that the caller must have been Kandie. She became glad that she trusted her husband to tell her himself, if he felt it was necessary for her to know. It would have been disastrous for her to spy on her husband. "What do you plan to do?" Bonita asked Kamal.

"Nothing," Kamal replied. "I will just watch her and see whatever she wants to do."

The following day, Kandie called Kamal again just as he closed for work. Kamal decided to pick the call.

"Hi Kandie. What's up?" Kamal stated in a mellow tone trying to hide his annoyance.

However, Kandie went on a rant. "I have been calling you and you have not been picking my calls. I sent you many text messages, but you did not reply."

"I am sorry Kandie, but I have been busy," Kamal responded.

"And I sent you a Giorgio Armani suit and you did not even acknowledge it," Kandie continued her ranting.

"Thank you for the suit. Are you happy now?"

"Is that all you are going to say?" Kandie asked in a disappointing tone.

"Did you want your suit back?" Kamal answered her with a question of his own.

Kandie paused. It was not the response she was expecting. Nonetheless, she summoned the courage to continue. "That is not why I called you. Are you too busy to have time for your only child?" Kandie asked him a rhetorical question.

However, referring to Kamal Junior as Kamal's only child infuriated Kamal beyond description as it made him remember the ordeal and the challenges that he went through with Bonita in order to have a child, the expenses they incurred and the loss of their twins. Therefore, he raised his voice while responding to Kandie.

"Don't ever call Junior my only child again," Kamal told Kandie.

"Oh, I see. Has your husband-snatching Mexican bimbo given birth to a baby for you?"

Kamal hung up his phone. He did not want to dignify Kandie's comment with an answer. However, Kandie called back, but Kamal did not pick her call. After the third call, Kamal picked up the phone and scolded kandie in very harsh words.

"Never ever refer to my wife like that again. Do I make myself clear?" Kamal yelled at Kandie as soon as he picked her call.

Kandie was surprised. She had never heard Kamal speak with such an angry tone like that before.

"You can defend her as much as you want. She and her family will soon find themselves in Mexico," Kandie predicted.

"So, you are the snake who called Immigration and Customs Enforcement agents on Bonita and her family?" Kamal inquired in anger.

Kandie refused to answer the question. Rather, she asked Kamal "Do you still want us to have joint custody for Kamal Junior?"

"What kind of stupid question is that?" Kamal replied her question with a question of his own.

"Fine. I will tell my lawyer to work to reverse the joint custody arrangement," Kandie threatened Kamal.

"Do whatever you want," Kamal replied and hung up the phone.

Leave me alone
When I met you
You were a sweet sixteen
When I discussed with you
You were a sweet treat
When I held your hand
You were awesome
When I walked with you
You were excellent
When I talked to you
You were a great delight

When I lodged with you
You were distinguished
When I wronged you
You were disappointed
When I appealed to you
You were unforgiving
When I needed you
You were bashful
Now that I don't want you
You are relentless in your pursuit
Please leave me alone
Please leave my wife alone
Please leave me and my wife alone.

Kandie was puzzled. The conversation had not gone as she had hoped. Kamal was not remotely as concerned about his son as she had expected. She had thought that his love for his son would make him do her bidding, but that has not panned out.

True to her promise, Kandie called her lawyer the following day and requested that the joint custody agreement be nullified, and her sole custody be reinstated.

"Please let me understand this," Attorney Pinocchioto sought clarification. "You want to stop your son's father from seeing your son anymore because he wasn't seeing your son as much as you expected him to be seeing him, right?"

"Yes, that is correct," Kandie confirmed.

"And you don't feel that such an action may actually be counter-productive?" Attorney Pinocchioto inquired again.

"Well, my son doesn't need him in his life," Kandie blurted out.

"Hmmm!" Attorney Pinocchioto sighed. "Maybe you should stop by the office later and we can proceed per your wishes."

After the lawyer hung up Kandie thought about the concern raised by her lawyer for a moment and decided that maybe she should still appeal to Kamal instead of cutting him off from the life of his son. She felt that time was of the essence but was not quite sure what she should do.

"Cutting between Kamal and Bonita seemed a daunting task. Their relationship felt like a fortress but there must be a way to get between them. There has got to be a way to create a crack," Kandie said to herself.

About four months after Bonita lost her twin pregnancy, she and Kamal returned to Dr Childlove to begin the process of another cycle of in-vitro fertilization. Although they were not happy from the memories of the unsuccessful pregnancy outcome, they had a ray of hope. The mood was not as tense when compared to the previous initial consultation. Nonetheless, there was a sense of loss because if the pregnancy had continued, it would have been at term at the time of the consultation.

"How have you guys been?" Dr Childlove asked Bonita and Kamal.

"Well, coping...as much as we can do," Bonita replied.

Kamal held Bonita's right hand and lovingly gently squeezed it in a reassuring solidarity, but did not speak.

"So, when was your last menstrual period?" Dr Childlove asked Bonita.

"I haven't seen my period since then," Bonita replied.

"Hmmm!" Dr Childlove sighed and wore a puzzled look.

"What?" Bonita asked with some anxiety in her voice.

"It is not unusual for menstruation to be delayed following spontaneous abortion or childbirth for some women," Dr Childlove explained. "It is related to hormone levels returning to normal and the physiological state returning to baseline. For some people also, when they lose weight rapidly or if they are under a lot of stress, their menstrual cycle may be affected."

"Well, I have not lost any weight...but as per stress, well..em...em.. you know.." Bonita tried to explain.

Kamal gently squeezed Bonita's hands again to establish his supportive presence and then remarked "we will be fine doc."

When situation matters not

Whether I am standing in Vienna, Austria
Or sitting down in Vienna, Virginia
Whether I am jogging in Alexandria, Virginia
Or imagining life in Alexandria, Egypt

Whether I am passing the night in Indiana
Or enjoying vacation in India
Whether I am tasting delicacies in Lagos
Or simply exploring the landscape in Laos
Whether I am on Broadway in Ney York City
Or just stuck in traffic on New York Avenue in DC
One thing that has persistently remained the same
Is that I am always happy with my lady, my dame
She is my wife
The joy of my life

Bonita, my love
I will always be with you
I will always be here with you
I will always be here for you

"How do you feel though?" Dr Childlove addressed Bonita while making eye contact with her.

"I just feel a little tired. Otherwise, I am fine," Bonita replied.

Dr Childlove then proceeded to examine Bonita. While examining her abdomen on the examining table, Dr Childlove sighed. This worried Bonita.

"What's wrong?" Bonita asked Dr Childlove.

"Your uterus has not fully involuted...I mean...your uterus has not shrunk down completely to its non-pregnant state," Dr Childlove explained.

"Why?" Bonita asked.

"We are about to find out now," Dr Childlove replied as he pulled the ultrasound machine in his office closer to the examining table. "When was the last time you urinated?"

"About three hours ago. Why?" Bonita replied looking puzzled.

"Great. I want to do a quick ultrasound evaluation of your abdomen," Dr Childlove replied.

Kamal started feeling uneasy where he was sitting, and he interlocked his fingers of both hands. His mind drew a blank and his anxiety level started rising.

Dr Childlove began the ultrasound examination by

applying a cold gel to the probe and warning Bonita that it may feel cold.

"My oh my!" Dr Childlove remarked unconsciously because of his surprise finding.

"What?" Kamal and Bonita asked in unison.

"I can't believe this," Dr Childlove stated with a happy tone.

Bonita could see Dr Childlove's face and saw that he was happy at what he saw. Kamal did not understand what was going on, so he jumped to his feet as his anxiety shot through the roof.

"What is it doc?" Kamal asked with a lot of concern.

"Congratulations! Mr and Mrs Brown. You are expecting another set of twins." Dr Childlove explained.

Kamal was stunned.

Bonita was initially shocked but after a few seconds, she yelled "seriously?"

"Yes. Mrs Brown. Yes. You are pregnant," Dr Childlove affirmed.

"But I have not seen my period," Bonita remarked trying to make sense of the wonderful news she heard.

"Exactly! That is why you have not seen your period," Dr Childlove explained sounding so happy himself.

"Really?" Bonita asked a question that did not require an answer.

Kamal jumped for joy trying to process the great news that just unfolded.

"Let me show you," Dr Childlove beckoned to them to watch the ultrasound screen as he applied the probe back to Bonita's abdomen. "See here... this is the sac of the first child, this is the sac of the second child."

"Wow!" Kamal exclaimed unable to control himself. Although, all he saw was just shadow of some sort but his inner being was excited beyond description.

"How long have I been pregnant?" Bonita asked Dr Childlove.

"I can be exact because you did not see your period at all, but given the findings at ultrasound, I would say about 5 to 6 weeks," Dr Childlove suggested.

The drive back home was one of the happiest moments in the lives of Bonita and Kamal. It was a sharp contrast to when they were driving back home from the hospital after Bonita was discharged about four months previously. That time, they were sad, Bonita was crying while Kamal was trying to stay strong and kept fighting his tears. They barely spoke to each other during the sad drive back home having lost their twins.

This drive home was awesome! The couple repeatedly expressed their gratitude to the Almighty for the unexpected "gift." Bonita could not stop chatting with a lot of excitement in her voice. She kept wondering why she did not have any nausea or vomiting like she had during the first pregnancy. She talked and talked. Kamal did not say much. He just listened and listened.

It was profound joy in the Brown's household that day. For dinner, Kamal decided to order a take-away meal from *Kabob and Grill*, an Asian cuisine. Bonita remained excited and just kept talking and talking from joy. She talked so much and barely ate anything. Kamal felt he had to do something about it.

> **Author's Note:** If a husband and wife are eating together, what percentage of the food is generally consumed by the husband and what percentage of the food is generally consumed by the wife?

"By virtue of the power vested in me by nobody and as the father of these twins who have just boarded their flight in your womb, I am hereby ordering you to eat or I am going to feed you myself. This is not an empty threat," Kamal stated while making gesture as if he has a megaphone in his hand for the whole world to hear his fake threat.

Bonita shook her head, smiled, and replied, "Kamal, I dare you to feed me the grilled lamb."

She subsequently sat straight and opened her mouth.

True to his words, Kamal carried out his threat. He took a bite size of the grilled lamb chop and put it in Bonita's mouth. She chewed and swallowed it. She then asked for more, being selective of what she wanted. Kamal lovingly fed her the complete meal. In fact, the only reason why she drank the juice by herself was because there was no drinking straw for Kamal to use to put the drink in her mouth.

"Thank you very much darling. Now, I will appreciate you doing just that three times everyday until the babies arrive," Bonita remarked.

Kamal shook his head, rolled his eyeballs, and continued his food.

When the pregnancy reached thirty-four weeks by ultrasound, Bonita expressed that she is tired and can't wait for the babies to come out.

"You know it was your fault?" Kamal remarked.

"How?" Bonita inquired.

"You chose hens over penguins."

"Huh?" Bonita expressed surprise. She did not understand what Kamal was talking about.

"Do you remember when we were in Dr Childlove's office and he used a parable of emperor penguins……. but you preferred the comparison with hens?"

"Okay…and your point is…" Bonita asked.

"With the emperor penguins, the female lays the egg and pass it on to the male who then stay without food or water for about four months in the frigid cold winter to actually protect and hatch eggs while the female goes back into the sea to feed. However, in the parable you chose, hens produce and hatch the eggs themselves."

"Well said. No problem. Next time, we are going the route of emperor penguins," Bonita suggested.

"Too late baby. Too late. We have already established our pattern. You won and I lost," Kamal established.

"You are seriously not serious," Bonita concluded.

At thirty-eight weeks of pregnancy, Bonita underwent an elective cesarean section by Dr Childlove and delivered a boy and a girl. The couple were ecstatic. The children were named Jack and Jacklyn.

Part Three

Upholding Upheaval:
The story of Ray

Part Three: Section One:
Who is pregnant?

"**D**esiree! Why are you addressing me in this condescending manner?" Ray yelled at his wife.

"I am sick and tired of being a homemaker. I am tired of waiting on you. I need to do something worthwhile with my life too," Desiree yelled back at her husband.

Ray was stunned. Nothing his wife was saying made any sense to him. She kissed him goodbye earlier that morning when he went for a job interview in Mount Vernon Community College in Northern Virginia to be a part-time professor for an additional income for the family. He just arrived home only for the wife to be yelling at him as soon as he entered the house. She did not even respond to his greetings let alone ask him what happened at the interview.

Desiree continued her ranting "I am not your doormat to be stepped upon as you wish. I am not an incubator that all I can do is to bring forth your babies. I am an intelligent smart woman. I am definitely not your baby caddy and I refuse to go down in history simply as Attorney Ray Marshall's wife."

Ray remained puzzled. He still couldn't make much sense from what Desiree was saying to him. Yes, she is pregnant, but he knew that it wasn't hormonal disturbance of any sort that was making Desiree go on this ill-advised tirade against him. He has never referred to her as any of the nonsensical depiction that Desiree was stating. He tried to calm the situation down.

"Baby, did something happen when I left the house?" Ray inquired in a partially subdued tone.

"Don't ever baby me again!" Desiree yelled at her husband again.

Ray started feeling angry. At this point he was not sure what he could do to figure out was going on with Desiree. When he realized that his efforts to calm Desiree down were unsuccessful, Ray simply left the house to try and calm himself down. He ate dinner in a restaurant while he was out and came back home very late in the night. He did not speak to Desiree at all.

That fateful Tuesday started and ended badly for Desiree on all fronts. She kissed her husband goodbye early in the morning and wished him the very best in his job interview to be a part-time professor at Mount Vernon Community College. Later that morning, Lisa accidentally spilled her breakfast chocolate drink on her homework which was due to be turned in to the teacher that morning. She wouldn't stop crying while she was being taken to school. Desiree tried her best to console and comfort her, but her efforts proved abortive as she did not stop crying all the way to school. Desiree returned home to hurriedly get ready and go to her antenatal appointment. She noticed that her front passenger side tire was flat. She had to call for road services assistance through her car insurance to come to her aid at home to change her tire. She called the doctor's office that she will be running late. She eventually arrived at her appointment about one hour and thirty minutes late. As promised, the obstetrician in charge of her high-risk pregnancy decided to fit her into the schedule rather than rescheduling her because it was an important visit to monitor her health status, evaluate the status of her high-risk pregnancy and perform an ultrasound since she was almost six months into her pregnancy. This made her wait longer at the doctor's office than she envisaged. To worsen the situation, when she was eventually called into the consultation room to be seen, the young physician who was doing his residency in obstetrics and gynecology in the hospital presented Desiree's case to the senior attending in charge of her care just outside the consulting room. He said that Desiree has high risk pregnancy and she will soon be an *"elderly grand multipara."* He said this within an earshot of Desiree. Although this medical terminology description merely means that Desiree is older than thirty-five years of age and at the end of her pregnancy, she would have delivered five or more babies. Desiree was bewildered and felt that she was being ridiculed as an elderly pregnant grandmother. Rather than bringing it up for it to be explained to her, Desiree blamed herself for her pregnancy because at age thirty-eight, pregnancy was definitely not on her to-do-list. She felt that the postgraduate trainee was simply rubbing in the insult for her. After all, if she did not forget her birth control pills when Ray travelled, she would not be in this position to be ridiculed as an elderly pregnant patient. The Attending Physician-in-charge noticed that Desiree was quite quiet, but he attributed it to the longer wait she had to endure. Therefore, he apologized to her for the long wait even though Desiree was the one who was late to her appointment. He performed the ultrasound and revealed the sex of the baby to Desiree.

After leaving the hospital, Desiree was in a hurry to get to the school to pick her children up. She did not want to incur charges for late pick up because her children were not in the aftercare program. At the intersection of Veterans way and Washington Boulevard, a guy driving a mid-size car in front of her was on his cellphone and did not pay attention to the traffic light. He slowed down and did not move fast enough to cross the intersection when the light was green. Subsequently, he accelerated when the light was yellow to cross the intersection. Desiree was in a hurry, so she committed to cross the intersection and crossed it as the light turned red. She felt that she saw a flash of light behind her. Then she remembered that there was a traffic camera at that notorious intersection. Desiree became mortified with the reality that she may get a photo of her car and a hundred-dollar bill for this traffic infraction. If it happens that way, a traffic citation bill is going to come in Ray's name again because the car was registered in his name. No doubt, Ray will be angry and accuse her of being a bad driver. She recently got a stupid speeding ticket on I-295 parkway. There were no construction cones on the road, and it became a speed trap for all motorists. There was no conspicuously displayed reduction in the usual speed from 55 miles per hour to 40 miles per hour. The police charged her $200 for going at 53 miles per hour. The breakdown of the charges was $100 for the speeding and $100 penalty for speeding in a construction zone. Suffice to say that Ray was angry to pay that bill. He accused her of not paying attention. That was only a month previously.

When she got home after picking her children from school, she rapidly made sandwiches for them and started preparing for dinner. Suddenly, the phone rang. It was Susan, her best friend since high school.

Susan asked Desiree questions in close succession without waiting for a response, "How are you? How was the doctor's visit and is the baby kicking you well?"

Desiree replied, "I feel like kicking the baby myself."

"Why? What happened?"

"I just came back home. It had been quite a challenging and unpleasant day for me," Desiree recounted the day's events for Susan.

"Is the baby okay though?" Susan inquired showing genuine concern.

Desiree responded, "the baby is doing okay, but the postgraduate doctor is a jerk."

"You mean… he is a jerk …kinda like a jerk chicken, the Jamaica treat," Susan asked jokingly.

"I am serious!" Desiree raised her voice. She then informed Susan that the doctor referred to her as an elderly pregnant grandma.

Susan sighed.

"What?" Desiree asked.

"I was just thinking…Hmmm!" Susan started talking and then sighed again.

"C'mon Susan!" Desiree exclaimed. "What were you thinking?"

"I was just thinking about how the future is always hard to predict," Susan continued.

"What did you mean?" Desiree inquired.

"I mean. Look at you! Who would have predicted that this is the condition that you would be?" Susan charged.

"I am not following you," Desiree expressed her being puzzled.

"Who would have predicted that you would be a housewife? That you will not be working and contributing positively to the society except by bringing forth babies for your husband. I mean...you are not the outspoken community organizing *Director Desiree* the valedictorian we knew in High School. You are not even a fainting shadow of the honor student you were in College," Susan emphasized.

"Hmmm!" Desiree sighed as she started feeling like a failure.

"I don't mean to annoy you or anything, but you are my best friend. I know it is true that educated women don't give birth to a busload of children in this day and age. However, let's face it... it is simply because you lack economic empowerment. You shouldn't be in a position where a trainee doctor will be insulting you as an elderly pregnant grandma. Honestly, I would think that if one of us will be a Chief Executive Officer of a fortune five hundred company, that would be you...but now... I mean...you have four children now and another one is on the way and you are Ms Ray Marshall....which is good but I am sure that this is not the future you went to school for, right?"

"Hmmm!" Desiree sighed again. She paused for a short while as her blood continued to boil. She then answered with a profound disappointment in her voice, "Yea. I guess you are right."

"Well, look at me! I mean...I leave in my own apartment. I may not be married, and I have no children, but I am happy with my life. At the present time, I am debating where to go for my vacation this year. I am trying to decide whether to go to Cancun, Istanbul, Barcelona or Thailand. I am leaning towards Thailand.... thinking that if I go there, I may finally learn how to pronounce the full name of the capital."

"Isn't that just Bangkok?" Desiree asked with a snap.

"No, my friend. That is why we need to get out more often. The full name of the capital is made up of 168 alphabets and it is the longest name of a place according to the record books. According to this tourist flyer, Bangkok is from *Bang Makok*, which means *Place of Olive Plums*, but the full official title of the city is actually *Krung Thep Mahanakhon Amon Rattanakosin Mahinthara Yuthaya Mahadilok Phop Noppharat Ratchathani Burirom Udomratchaniwet Mahasathan Amon Piman Awatan Sathit Sakkathattiya Witsanukam Prasit.*"

"Hmmm!" Desiree sighed feeling deflated.

Susan continued "For me, life is good. I have my own 401(k) retirement account. Right now, I am planning to invest in real estate properties apart from my investment in the stock market. I drive my own car and I get home when I want. I don't have to rush anywhere to please any man or wait on him or clean after him. Nothing like that at all."

"Hmmm!" Desiree sighed again.

"I get it that your husband is doing a good job of taking care of you and your children, but what if something happens? I know he is a nice guy and I hope he doesn't cheat on you. However, I have heard stories of professors who leave their wives for their graduate students ...but again, I respect your choices...Sorry Desiree, I have to go. I am starving and my *Lean Cuisine* entree is done in the microwave. Talk to you later my friend."

"Okay Susan. Thanks. Talk to you later," Desiree replied as she hung up the phone.

Desiree had just hung up the phone when she heard the engine of Ray's car in the driveway. Her blood boiled over as he entered the house leading to her venting her spleen on her poor husband. Ray was actually excited to come home to inform Desiree that he got the job "on the spot" at the interview. Unfortunately, all he met was an incredibly angry wife who was blaming him for her apparent underachieving life.

For four days, there was no meaningful conversation between Ray and Desiree. Ray was in no mood for a fight, but he remained angry about the way Desiree treated him. In the afternoon on Saturday, Ray decided to watch television while sitting on the couch. He flipped through a few channels before the re-run of a newlywed couple's game show caught his attention. In the episode that was on, the couple were being asked things about the other spouse. Ray watched as the wife of one of the contestants became visibly upset that her husband forgot the name of the restaurant where they had their first meal together as a married couple. Ray mused out of despondency. "These lovebirds have no idea what is in stock for them in a few months and years," Ray said to himself.

Suddenly, his thought was interrupted by Desiree.

"I am going back to school to get my Master of Business Administration degree and I am going to get a job afterwards," she declared to Ray. Desiree declared her future plan while standing between Ray and the television screen and thereby, obstructing his view.

Ray tried not to be upset but shifted sideways while making hand gesticulation for Desiree to move to the side.

"Whatever!" He replied registering his indifference to what Desiree said and continued to watch the game show.

**What is a house plant missing? Fresh breeze?
Warm sunlight? Or animals peeing on it?**

About twenty minutes later, his thought was interrupted again.

"Daddy! Daddy!" Lisa called him.

"What!" Ray exclaimed, feeling disturbed. He turned his head to the right side and saw Lisa standing next to the couch trying to get his attention. The innocent look in her eyes soften his heart mollifying some of his pent-up anger against Desiree, her mother. However, there was a familiar tone to the way she called him. The last time she called him like that was just three days previously when she called him to tell him that she lost a tooth.

"Sorry to hear that you lost your tooth. Are you hurting?"

"No dad," Lisa replied.

"Is it bleeding?"

No, dad. I am fine," Lisa expressed.

"Great," Ray concluded but Lisa did not move. So, he asked her. "is there something else?"

Lisa looked at the floor to avoid making eye contact and replied in a soft voice "Mum asked me to collect my gift from you."

"What gift? For what?"

"For my lost tooth," Lisa replied.

"Let me get this straight. Your mum told you to ask me for money to give you as a gift because you lost a tooth?"

"Yes dad."

"Do you really expect me to pay for your tooth?"

Lisa nodded in affirmation.

"I pay for the milk and cheese to make your teeth strong whether it a country like American or Swiss, or a town like cheddar or a structure like cottage or a person like Jack."

At that time, Desiree who had been listening to their conversation unbeknown to Ray interjected. "C'mon Ray, remember the tooth fairy?"

Ray faced Desiree and responded, "remember that the tooth fairy is a lady, not a man."

Desiree shook her head disappointingly that Ray did not play along.

Ray ignored her and faced Lisa, "talk to your mum in the evening. She may be able to get you the phone number of the tooth fairy."

Desiree simply took Lisa's left hand and they walked away with disappointment written boldly on Lisa's face.

Ray hoped that his father-daughter conversation with Lisa will be different from what happened three days previously. Therefore, he sat upright to give Lisa his attention.

"Can I ask you a question?" Lisa asked her father.

"Well, you just did," Ray replied in a jovial tone.

"No, I didn't," Lisa replied.

"You said... 'can I ask you a question,' right?"

"Yes daddy," Lisa concurred.

"Well, that was a question," Ray explained with a smirky smile.

"So, can I ask now?" Lisa inquired.

"Go on," Ray submitted.

"Where do babies come from?"

"Wow!" Ray exclaimed. The question caught him completely off-guard. After a couple of uneasy seconds, Ray replied with a question, "have you asked mummy?"

"Yes daddy," Lisa replied.

"So, what did she say?" Ray inquired.

"She said to ask you," Lisa answered.

Ray wondered why Desiree passed the buck. She should have explained to her daughter herself. After all, she is the one who is pregnant and carrying a baby.

"Go and ask your mummy again," Ray suggested to Lisa.

However, before Lisa could leave, Desiree walked into the living room and joined their presence.

"You can ask your daddy again. He knows the answer," Desiree retorted. Quite unknown to Ray, Desiree had been listening to the conversation between him and Lisa.

Lisa turned her attention to Ray.

Ray thought of telling her that babies come from a special section in the back store of the *Family Superstore* or *Babies R Us,* but a part of him felt that Lisa was too smart for that and that delay strategy is not likely to work. So, he tried to dodge the question again by tickling Lisa in her belly making her giggle.

After a few minutes of giggling, Desiree could not take it anymore.

"Lisa!"

"Yes, mummy"

"You do know that daddy has not yet answered your question, right?" Desiree reminded her in order to frustrate Ray's efforts to escape the question.

"Ooh!" Lisa exclaimed and stopped giggling. She then looked at Ray with disappointment written on her face.

Ray sighed. "Do you want some ice-cream?" Ray asked Lisa.

"Yes daddy," Lisa replied smiling.

Ray tried to get up from the couch to go to the kitchen for a timely distraction from answering the uneasy question. Desiree put her hand on his right shoulder effectively keeping him on the couch.

"I will get her the ice-cream later," Desiree remarked. "Daddy, please go ahead and answer the question."

Ray felt trapped. He looked at Desiree with a fake smile and followed it up with a stern gaze that clearly stated, "why are you doing this to me?"

Desiree ignored his facial expression. Rather, she faced Lisa and remarked "daddy is going to answer your question now my dear."

Ray threw Desiree a "you are throwing me under the bus" look which she promptly and conveniently ignored.

At that moment, Bryan and Paige walked into the living room. Patricia started wondering what was going on. So, she joined them too. The setting felt overwhelming for Ray but there was no way out. He must answer the question, "where do babies come from?"

"Where do babies come from?" Ray repeated the question loudly. He was wondering where to begin. Patricia and Paige started laughing.

"Go away!" Ray yelled at them in a jovial manner, but they did not leave. They continued to laugh. Desiree started laughing too. Bryan was just smiling. Ray did not find it funny and squeezed his face in a fake frown.

Ray recalled when Bryan asked him the same question a few years previously, he simply told him that "babies come from the tummies of their mummies." That was all he had to say, and the question ended there. Quickly, he reached out for this time-tested answer.

"Babies come from the tummies of their mummies," Ray answered with confidence.

"How did they get there?" Lisa followed it up with another question.

"What!" Ray exclaimed. He was hoping that his initial answer would have been enough like what happened with Bryan. He looked at Desiree with a "please bail me out face" which she ignored. Ray closed his eyes briefly as if he was looking for the answer in the inner recess of an abandoned attic in his brain. He summoned the courage to be truthful and simple at the same time.

"Do you know the difference between boys and girls?" Ray asked Lisa.

"Boys are annoying and dirty," Lisa replied.

"And girls talk too much," Bryan chimed immediately as if he was defending the reputation all boys.

"I mean in terms of ...em....em......you know...biology..." Ray struggled with his choice of words.

"Did you mean their private parts?" Patricia jumped in laughing.

Ray initially felt embarrassed by Patricia's comment, but it suddenly dawned on him that it was a great start. So, he picked it up from there.

"You know that the private parts of boys and girls are different, right?"

"Yes daddy," Lisa replied lowering her gaze out of shyness.

"Do you know why they are called private parts?"

Lisa did not answer. She stayed quiet.

Ray continued "They are called private because they are to be kept private. That is... they are to be kept away so that other people don't look at them or touch them. So, people should not take photographs of their private parts. Do you understand?"

"Yes daddy" Lisa replied.

"So, as they grow older, a boy will become a man and a girl will become a woman. When they get married, their bodies and their private parts come together, and their gifts then forms into a baby. The baby then grows inside the mother for nine months," Ray explained.

"How does the baby come out?" Lisa asked again.

Ray looked at Desiree and smiled while making a "the ball is in your court" gesture with his hands.

Desiree shook her head in disbelief that Ray was passing the buck again. Finally, she responded "After nine months of growing in the mummy's tummy, the baby usual come out through mummy's private part. However, if there is a problem, the doctors can do operation to bring the baby out of the mummy's belly."

Ray then turned to Lisa, "do you understand it now?"

"Yes. Thanks daddy. Thanks mummy."

"Speaking of baby, do you want mummy to have a baby girl or a baby boy?" Ray asked Lisa.

But before Lisa could respond, Patricia jumped in again.

"Absolutely, I want a baby sister!"

Ray turned to her and asked her "why?"

"Boys are very annoying and these two are enough," Patricia replied.

"What about you Paige and Bryan? Do you want a baby brother or baby sister?" Ray asked them.

"Baby sister," Paige replied.

"Definitely baby sister," Bryan responded.

Ray was surprised at the uniformity of their answers. "Why?" he asked them.

"We are okay in our room. We don't need another person to share our room," Paige responded.

Ray turned to Bryan who nodded in affirmation.

"Lisa, do you vote for a baby sister or a baby brother?" Ray asked her.

"I want a baby sister so that I can play with her," Lisa replied.

"Interesting! All of you want your mummy to deliver a baby girl albeit for different reasons."

"What about you daddy?" Lisa asked Ray.

"I want twins. A boy and a girl," Ray answered.

"Not happening dad," Patricia commented.

"Why did you say that?" Ray asked her.

"Mummy already told us that there is only one baby in there," Patricia explained.

"And you don't think that there is a chance for another baby to get in there also…to make it…kinda like… buy one, get one free?" Ray asked Patricia with tongue in cheek.

Patricia shook her head and rolled her eyeballs. "Seriously? C'mon dad. We know it is too late."

"Alright, in that case, I will vote for a baby girl too," Ray made his choice.

It then dawned on Ray that Desiree is likely to already know whether they were having a baby boy or girl from the ultrasound performed a few days earlier when she went for her ante-natal care. However, because she was mad at him for no good reason that day, they had not discussed the pregnancy issues at all.

"I wonder if your mummy wanted a baby boy or a baby girl," Ray commented hoping that Desiree will take the bait and simply tell them. Instead, Desiree turned and started going towards the kitchen. All the children followed her to inquire whether they were getting their wishes of a baby sister.

"So, what are you willing to do to bribe me into telling you whether you are having a baby brother or sister?"

Paige turned and started heading back to his room. The information was not that important enough for him to sacrifice anything for it.

"I will do the dishes tonight," Patricia volunteered.

"But you are already supposed to do the dishes," Desiree reminded her.

"I know mum. However, this time, I will do it with a smile."

Desiree chuckled. "What about you Bryan?"

"I will eat my dinner."

"And were you not planning to eat dinner before?"

"Okay mum. I will eat my vegetables too."

"C'mon guys you are not offering me a good deal. What about you Lisa?"

"I will play with the baby."

Desiree shook her head in disbelief. "You guys did not offer me anything!"

"P-L-E-A-S-E!!!" Bryan and Lisa shouted in unison.

"Okay. We are having a baby girl!" Desiree finally gave in.

"Yay!" Lisa shouted and ran to inform Ray in the living room.

Ray continued to watch television in the living room flipping the channels very often while pondering on the implications of what Desiree told him she was going to do immediately after childbirth. He felt sick to his stomach. He heard the determination in her voice and saw the fire of defiance in Desiree's eyes. Ray was convinced that a major disaster will be knocking on the door of his household. It was not about him. He was sure that he could take care of himself. It was about the children. He felt that their mother wanted to misplace her priority for self-aggrandizement.

"Why is Desiree this bad?" Ray asked himself. He began to feel that he married the worst of wives, at least when compared to Bonita and Eva. Bonita seems to be in a class of her own but even Eva must have been a forgiving, nice woman. Ray recalled his conversation with his friends when Kamal had asked him if he had ever appealed to Desiree to forgive him for any errors, mistakes, blunders.... anything and everything ....at all that he might have done that was making her so mean to him.

"Never. Why would I? She is the one who is always wrong. She denies me my right. She maltreats me while I keep doing my duties to her. C'mon! I still take care of her kids," Ray had replied.

"You can't be this blind. Even bats see at night," Kamal commented.

"Look here my friend. Desiree always do bad stuff to me deliberately," Ray remarked.

"And you never did anything that you shouldn't have done?" Kamal asked with sarcasm.

"Rarely. Well, maybe just once. At most, maybe twice," Ray clarified.

"Or may be thrice or ten times or two thousand times...

like ..in a day?" Kamal countered while shaking his head.

"I know that I am the S.I. unit of gentility, the epitome of easy going, the hallmark of being nice and the perfect example of being a gentleman," Ray asserted.

Adam suddenly chuckled which made his friends wonder what was going on in his befogged mind.

Adam then narrated, "I remembered one day when Eva and I got into an argument, which was very uncommon for us, because I am the real gentleman...."

"Of course, you are," Kamal remarked with tongue in cheek. "Nobody is like Ray, who is a flawless fake gentleman."

Ray simply shook his head and ignored both of them.

"Anyway, we were arguing about something and.....a little out of desperation... because she seemed to be winning the argument, I accused Eva of marrying me because of money," Adam recalled.

"That's interesting," Ray remarked. "I never went that low before."

Adam ignored Ray's comment and continued, "Eva and I were yelling at each other while arguing about something. After sometime, she just waived her hand and decided to walk away. Then I remarked that she did not love me anyway. She just married me for money. Hearing what I said made her stop dead in her track. It was as if my assertion made her change her mood from anger to sarcasm. She turned and faced me walking back. "Money? What money?" she asked in close succession. "You? Money? She asked as if those two words do not belong together. When I married you, you did not have your own apartment. You did not even have a bed!" Eva recalled.

Kamal and Ray chuckled. "You did not have a bed when you got married?" Ray inquired.

"Her statement was not true. We had a bed. It just belonged to the hospital that I was working for at that time. We lived in a furnished apartment that belonged to the hospital. Yes, it had a bed," Adam tried to explain.

"Oh, I see," Kamal remarked with tongue in cheek and hit Ray on the elbow indicating that he was being sarcastic.

Adam ignored him and continued, "Eva then kept

reminding me, 'you did not have a car!' but I corrected her immediately that I had a car, it was just not with me yet."

"And she did not know that you have a car?" Ray became inquisitive.

"No. I mean… what I was referring to ….was that my car was already manufactured. It was just with the current owner at that time. I bought a 1987 Chevy Cavalier later. So, my car was already existing, it was just not with me yet."

"Oh, I see. It was the same argument for your house, money in your bank account et cetera. They were just somewhere else," Ray pretended to understand and agree with Adam's argument.

"Anyway, I changed the direction of the conversation and asserted that she married me because of my potential for success."

"And I am sure she gave you a befitting response," Kamal opined while chuckling.

"She did alright …..as she started walking away again."

"What did she say?" Ray asked.

"Your potential? Of course, yes…..and ten years later, it is still nothing but a potential. Please blame my great… outstanding…wonderful foresight! I wonder when this potential of yours will become a real "Action Potential" that can make something worthwhile to happen… making air quotes while saying *action potential*.

"Ouch!" Ray exclaimed. "That was below the belt."

"No. I won in the end," Adam remarked beaming with masculine pride.

"How so?" Ray became curious.

"As she turned and started leaving, I looked at her from behind and she looked inviting as she was walking away. So, I ran to her and slapped her lovingly on her butt and ran away. She tried to chase me, but she couldn't catch me, and we started laughing. She promised that she will get me back, but she did not do anything that I can remember," Adam concluded.

Ray's mind came back to the present as he changed the channel of the television once again. He mused to himself saying, "normal couples can always find ways to diffuse tension if they really wanted to stay together. They just have to be committed to it and learn to overlook each other's flaws. Why is Desiree so bad? She is just a hot headed, unnecessarily difficult, and unappreciative woman. I need to move on and find my happiness elsewhere."

True to her words, Desiree enrolled in a Master of Business Administration Program and started her initial classes online for the Graduate Management Admission Test (GMAT) before the baby was born. Her determination to succeed was all that matters. She stopped giving the same level of attention to her children the way she used to do previously. Nothing else matters now. Only her career and anything that promotes it.

Desiree stopped staying at home on the weekends. She would rather go to the library to study, leaving her children with instructions that were never followed. This forced Ray to be the only person at home to watch over the children, a position he has never been in over 15 years of marriage.

After a few weeks, Ray started feeling more like a house help rather than a husband in his own home. He could not help remembering that he has always been the one who pays all the bills since they tied the nuptial knot. On one occasion on a weekend afternoon, Ray heard some noise and struggle in the boy's bedroom. He entered their room. Ray could not believe his eyes as per how dirty and upside down the room was. They had books all over the floor and dirty clothes were everywhere. The fact that the boys were fighting over trifles did not bother him as much as how horrible their room looked. He told Paige and Bryan to tidy up their room immediately. He felt the girls would be better. Nonetheless. He decided to check on them too. Their room arguably looked worse. Ray felt he was in a 'dumpster with a door' in the middle of his house. There were clothes everywhere, the beds were not made, and there were sheets of paper everywhere. Even though the children have been instructed not to eat in their bedrooms, it was very obvious that they have been flouting this law. There were empty cans of soda, empty wrappers of cookies, potato chips and other junk foods of different colors practically everywhere. Ray scolded

Patricia and Lisa and they pointed accusatory fingers at each other. Ray instructed them to clean their room and make it presentable and worthy of been called a bedroom. He gave his children thirty minutes to clean their rooms making it clear to all of them that he was coming back to inspect their rooms with stern punishment if their rooms were still horrible. True to his words, thirty minutes later, he went back to check their rooms. The boys' and the girls' rooms showed evidence that somebody did something, but he noted that he did not see many activities coming out of the rooms. He knew that they must have only done some cosmetic work. While in the boys' room, Ray decided to look under the bed. He found a pile of dirty clothes and all the dirt he saw earlier. Apparently, all they did was to pack all the dirty clothes and other wastes and hid them under the bed. They then laid their beds. Ray was livid. He scolded and grounded them for a week. He then went to the girls' room and could readily sense that they must have done the same thing. However, when he looked under the bed, there was nothing there. He only found some shoes. His sixth sense told him that the dirt must still be somewhere in the room. He did not feel that the girls did a better job either. So, he proceeded to the wardrobe. As soon as he opened it, dirty clothes rained on the floor like pus from a ripe boil that has just been punctured. Ray was very angry with his daughters. He scolded and grounded them for a week too. He then gave all the children two hours to completely clean their rooms and vacuum the floors. They were to report back to him when the tasks have been completed. After about an hour and half of peace and quiet, Ray suddenly heard a loud argument between Patricia and Paige regarding who will use the vacuum cleaner first. Ray was angry and he directed his annoyance to Desiree, their mother who he felt was neglecting her real duties at home.

Authors note: Ray sees his children as parasites and pests who are depriving him of his wife. Desiree sees her children as career killers who did not let her develop her potential and contribute meaningfully to the society. The larger question is, "how do we measure individual's contribution to the society? Who determines who has contributed more to the society? Individuals? Religious institutions? Government? Socialites? Talking heads on the television? or members of the single mother's network?"

When Desiree came back from the library in the evening, Ray sought audience with her for them to discuss and strategize how the family is not going to suffer too much on account of Desiree's career pursuit. However, Desiree accused Ray of just wanting to be a stumbling block in her path of success. This infuriated Ray, and he said to her, "you are only misplacing your priorities!"

On December 31st at 7 pm, Desiree noted that her water broke. She informed Ray and called Nana to help them look after the other children while they are away to the hospital for the delivery of their baby. After Nana arrived, they started heading for the hospital.

Desiree had packed 'baby items' in two new special 'baby bags' for a few weeks in anticipation of the delivery. Ray picked the two 'baby bags' and remarked. "Today is the 'D – Day!'

"I told you to stop saying D-Day. My baby is not invading our house!" Desiree remarked with muted anger.

"The 'D' is for Delivery," Ray corrected her.

"I know but every time you say D-Day, all I can think of is invasion," Desiree explained.

"You should expand your thinking process instead….you know….in order to accommodate more things and diverse opinions," Ray suggested.

"Or you can simply stop saying a stupid D-Day regarding our baby!" Desiree yelled.

"What are you yelling for? Must you be obnoxious all the time?" Ray asked Desiree raising his voice too.

Nana cleared her throat and coughed to mediate in the argument of the couple without saying a word. It was enough to register to Ray and Desiree to stop their argument.

They headed for the car as Nana continued to pray for a safe delivery. Desiree got in the back seat of the car. Ray did not talk to her throughout the thirty-minute drive to the hospital. They reported directly to the labor ward and completed the in-processing by 9:30 PM. All her previous pregnancies were normal deliveries and they generally lasted between seven to ten hours.

While the midwife was attending to Desiree and checking the well-being of the baby with a baby monitor, Ray remarked jokingly to the midwife "please let the baby come out at 12.01 AM so that our baby will be the first baby of the year in the United States."

The midwife chuckled but did not reply.

Ray continued "It is amazing how much difference a few minutes can make. If a child is born on December 31st at 11:59 PM, nobody reckons with the birth. There is no award or special gifts for being the last baby of the year. However, if the baby was born 2 minutes later, the baby becomes the first baby of the year with media coverage and gifts."

"What did you...?" Desiree wanted to get in the conversation but the pain of labor which had become more intense made her cut off her question.

"The labor progressed faster than Ray expected and by 11:35 PM, the entire delivery team were in their labor room suite ready for the baby. A part of Ray really wished the baby will be born at 12:01 AM but the baby was not watching the clock.

Amanda was born at 11:50 PM on December 31st. She cried immediately after she was born. Ray mused to himself ...secretly wishing that he could spank her, not to make her cry, but for not waiting just ten more minutes before coming out...maybe it was Desiree's fault...she should have held off pushing.... for just ten more minutes. He then chuckled as per how silly that thought was.

About one hour later after the room had been tidied and Desiree has been freshened, the baby was brought back and given to the happy parents. Ray looked at Desiree adoringly and kissed her forehead. He then remarked "this baby is going to grow up being upset with you for not waiting for ten minutes before you pushed her out."

"No problem at all," Desiree replied. "Every time, she brings it up, I will surely give her a ten-minute 'timeout' for not waiting ten more minutes before she broke her water."

Two days later, Ray, Desiree and baby Amanda came home from the hospital. It heralded the beginning of a new challenge and the challenge of a new beginning.

Part Three: Section Two:
Who is suffering?

A new world of challenges erupted when Ray took up a part-time faculty position in Mount Vernon Community College to teach *Law and Ethics*. On his first day in the college, he went to the cafeteria and saw an Automatic Teller Machine (ATM) for his bank. Ray decided to withdraw some cash since he was not going to be incurring a surcharge. When he finished, he saw that there was a young attractive lady behind him waiting to use the ATM too. Ray smiled and said to her, "I left some money in there for you."

The young lady smiled but did not say anything.

Ray, then said, "you should say thank you."

Then she chuckled and replied in form of a question with a classic South Carolina accent, "and if I don't?"

"Then I will withdraw all the money from the ATM."

"Really? With all due respect sir, if you work here, you do not make enough money to bankrupt an ATM."

Ray had no answer. He smiled, shook his head in agreement and remarked "well, you do have a point there." He then left the cafeteria and headed to Administrative building to meet Grace, the administrative assistant in charge of in-processing at the departmental level.

Grace is a gorgeous and incredibly beautiful young woman in her early thirties. Her voice was sonorous and seemed to have a ringing tone to it. She has a welcoming personality. Ray completed all the required paperwork. She issued him his office key led him to it.

The following day, Ray passed by Grace's office as her office was right across from the West elevator. She wore a fake frown.

"Hi Grace. Are you okay?"

"Nope!" Grace replied.

"What happened?"

"You didn't notice my eye shadows."

"I am sorry," Ray responded.

"Do you like my nails? I just got them done."

"I am so sorry. I generally don't pay attention to those things."

"Why?" Grace asked with a genuine surprise in her voice.

"Well…em…em…you know… the fact is that if I should pay attention to those things, one of two disasters will happen."

"Disasters?" Grace was puzzled.

"Yes. Disasters," Ray affirmed. "Number one, your husband will kill me or number two, my wife will kill me."

"Well, I am not married. So, no husband of mine is going to kill you."

"I am still a dead man anyway because my wife will kill me."

"Well, we won't tell her," Grace chuckled while rolling her eyeballs with a seductive smile.

Ray quickly changed the subject by passing a comment on the fountain in front of the quadrangle, "what a lovely fountain outside! Very nice design." Then, he quickly excused himself.

Subsequently, Ray consciously avoided the West elevator because the door of the elevator opens right in front of Grace's office. Ray persistently used the East elevator and then walk a fair distance to get to his office. He felt that it was a necessary precaution for him, akin to avoiding being blown apart on a mine field.

When Ray related this experience to his friends, they teased him.

"Let me get this straight, you chickened out!" Adam remarked.

"Call me chicken or turkey if you like. I was protecting

my career and my marriage. Even though it was a difficult undertaking because Desiree just doesn't get it. However, familiarity breeds…"

"Contempt!" Adam interjected.

"Well, it will breed contempt if she says '*no*' but it will breed children if she says '*yes.*' Nonetheless, familiarity breeds a 'C' word. I am not ready for whatever the 'C' word is," Ray clarified.

The summer school was particularly difficult for Ray because as the temperature warmed up, the clothes of the students either shrank or came off in their expression of fashion freedom. Ray felt he needed a refresher course on lowering his gaze too. He is a married man who is not getting enough attention from his wife and now must contend with three days of teaching young beauties who have no qualms with making a wanton display of their treasures. His emotional love challenge was quite a tough challenge. The problem was that he needed the additional income and this teaching gig fills his wallet with the much-needed extra money.

Fortunately for Ray, the *Law and Ethics* class itself was a lot of fun because he turned out to be a very good teacher. His private practice experience was always on display and he used real life cases for his examples. Although the course was compulsory, the students actually enjoyed the class. Unfortunately, the emotional deprivation suffered by Ray continued unabated. It was a revolving door of disaster. Desiree will say her patented, *"No! Leave me alone"* emotional abuses, he will try to work out and burn his emotions by taking out his frustration on the elliptical machine and treadmills in the gym but will end up seeing far more desirable single women in the gym. Then, he will go to school to teach flowers that are just getting to their prime bloom. If Ray thought that going to the gym when Desiree was not taking care of him was tough, going to teach in a community college when Desiree was not taking care of him was a whole lot tougher. Unfortunately, he needed the money. He just always had to ensure that he remained professional and safeguard himself.

Ray remembered a common statement attributed to three wise Japanese monkeys in a folklore advising everybody to "see no evil, hear no evil and speak no evil." Ray added that additional monkeys are needed to tell everybody to "do no evil, taste no evil, touch no evil, eat no evil, drink no evil, and don't be alone in a place with evil."

"Indeed, there is no room, no house, no street, no city, no county, no country, and no continent for a deprived man!" Ray lamented to himself. In order to protect himself from his fragile emotional challenges, Ray ensured that his office hours to meet with his students took place in the classroom and never behind closed doors. Ray knew that emotions roll on too wild when you are feeling vulnerable. He felt that he was always feeling deprived and his *vulnerability index* remained consistently astronomically high. He felt that he was always in a persistent state of emotional need that was not being fulfilled but Desiree just did not get it. This state is never sustainable to any man. It is just a matter of time before a catastrophe occurs. This is what he has been trying to avoid, but it seems inevitable.

The problems at home raged on like wildfire at the time of drought. These challenges ranged from mild to very serious. Desiree not doing her comfort duties to Ray was the peak of very serious. However, he still had to contend with many other family issues at home with the older children. He struggled, but he tried to rise to the occasion with taking care of Amanda too.

One evening after returning from his teaching assignment, Ray felt that the deprivation of love was getting too much for him to bear in the face of constantly running away from potential extra-marital succor he could pursue. He decided to quit the teaching job to minimize his *emotional fragility*. When he got home, he noticed that his mails were placed on the table for him. They were all too familiar. Bills! Bills! Bills! Just bills! Nothing but bills to pay. Unfortunately, all the bills kept going up. His salary as a lawyer has not kept up with his responsibilities and the rising cost of pretty much.... everything in his life. Ray opened the credit card statement. The bill was approximately fifty percent higher than the previous month's bill. Ray quickly changed his mind about quitting the teaching job. He shook his head in submission to his predicament. Rather than getting angry, he decided to pull Desiree's legs.

"Desiree! Desiree!!" Ray shouted from the living room.

"What?" Desiree responded.

'The baby is racking up the credit card bill. It seems you are using too many diapers."

"Well, babies poop, right?" Desiree retorted.

"I think you should reduce how much food she is eating so that she will have less poop. Less poop means less diapers, and less diapers means less credit card bill, right?"

Desiree did not bother to reply him.

After a few seconds, Ray spoke again. "An alternative is to potty train the baby so that she can use the toilet like everybody else. I am sure that process is cheaper."

Desiree initially thought to ignore him. Finally, she couldn't hold herself and she replied from the kitchen, "so, mister cost-saving genius, how do you plan to potty train a three-month old baby who cannot even sit down by herself?"

"It is a new day honey!" Ray replied. "This new generation of children do everything early. They operate I-pads with their eyes and write with their thumbs. I am sure that with the right motivation and encouragement, you can potty train her."

Desiree simply shook her head and did not respond.

The following day, on returning from picking Amanda up from the daycare center, Desiree gave Amanda to Ray to feed her with the breast milk she had pumped so that she could go and start preparing dinner.

Ray did as instructed but after a few minutes, he remarked... "Ewww" loudly.

"What happened?" Desiree asked as she started making her way from the kitchen to the living room where Ray and Amanda were sitting to see what occurred.

"Your baby just puked your breast milk on my shirt. It is disgusting!" Ray answered.

"Really?" Desiree responded as she got within an eyeshot of Ray and Amanda. Some white liquid regurgitation was on Ray's shirt.

"That is what you are complaining about?" Desiree asked Ray a rhetorical question. "Next time, you can go and get her another milk that is not disgusting. Better still you can feed her your own breast milk. I am sure that your breast milk is not disgusting."

Without waiting for an answer, she turned and started heading back to the kitchen.

"Not gonna happen!" Ray replied.

Desiree stopped as if she wanted to say something.

Ray continued, "I am staying away from getting milk from any human, animal or plant. The last time you asked me to buy milk ended in disaster. You were not appreciative."

Desiree simply shook her head and headed back to the kitchen.

Ray was recalling the milk purchase debacle which happened about two weeks previously. Desiree called him at work and asked him to get three gallons of milk on his way from the office. He thought it was a simple chore until he got to the supermarket to discover that there were so many different types of milk and did not know what to buy. Some rectangular packages of milk even have unusual writings on them like *Almond milk*, *Oat milk*, *Rice milk*, and *Soy milk*. It sounded funny to Ray who wondered when plants started breastfeeding. He was surprised to see that even within the same type of milk packaging, the milk scored different percentages of something 1% and 2%. Then there was one in a multicolored pack that was fifty percent of something and fifty percent of something else. Ray wondered what concoction was put in the pack that made them call it *half and half*. The worst part was that he did not have his reading glasses with him and could not read the tiny details on the labels. The wheat bread versus honey wheat bread catastrophe rose from the dead in his mind. He did not want a repeat of that mess. He promptly called Desiree in order to clarify what specific type of milk he should buy but she did not pick up. He left her a message on her voice mail. He also sent her a text message, but he did not get any response.

Ray became frustrated after waiting for three minutes in front of the standing row refrigerators housing different dairy products in the supermarket.

"Women always want to have phones and they want you to call them. However, when you call them, they never pick up. Why? Why? Why?" Ray complained to himself. "They buy the latest, the most expensive phones and then put their phones on silent or vibration modes. Their phones are then imprisoned in a corner of their handbags which contain everything in the world to dampen the vibrations from the phone. Even though they cost a fortune, their handbags are never on their hands. Yet, they still call them handbags. If only they will keep the handbags on their hands, there may be a slim a chance of feeling the vibration when they receive a phone call. Rather, the handbags will be on the table where there is no chance to know that anyone called."

Ray looked at his watch for the umpteenth time, he had been standing in the dairy isle for almost five minutes now. He could not take it anymore. He felt that women deliberately frustrate men. "When you are courting a woman, she will deliberately make you go through hoops. Women are always slow to make up their minds. The lame excuse is that they are trying to gauge your interest. Even if that is understandable during courtship, it is absolutely ridiculous for a married woman to be testing the patience of her husband and yet, they wonder why their husbands look so old soon after marriage!" Ray lamented to himself.

He called Desiree's phone again. It rang many times and went into her voicemail again. Ray did not bother to leave a message this time around. He simply hung up and concluded that Desiree just wanted to frustrate him deliberately.

Ray opened the refrigerator wondering which milk to pick. A part of him suggested to get whole milk only. At least, that means the milk is whole and complete. That way Desiree can add water to it in order to make it whatever percentage water she wanted. Another suggestion occurred to him and he decided to pick one whole milk, one 2% milk, one 1% milk and one skim milk. Yes, Desiree asked him to buy three gallons of milk, but he would have bought four gallons. He was convinced that it was a better strategy than buying only one type of milk. This is because if the chosen milk turned out to be the wrong one, he will be more upset with Desiree if she should complain in any way. At least, with the current strategy, one of the gallons of milk is likely to be the correct one. They will have to make do with the remaining three gallons of milk. Returning them is totally out of consideration.

When Ray got home, Desiree was not at home. Patricia noted that her dad was very upset. Ray lamented his experience to her regarding having to make that milky decision. Patricia took two gallons of milk from her father and held his hand.

"Sorry about that dad. Thank you for buying the milk," Patricia remarked.

The response from Patricia to Ray was magical! Ray felt very appreciated, and his anger dissipated immediately. Even Ray could not believe the impact that Patricia's gesture had on him. He felt happy. Out of the blues, he hugged her and said, "thank you my dear."

Patricia was surprised too. She did not see that coming. It felt weird that her dad will hug her and thank her...... just for thanking him. Little did she know that men love to be appreciated for what they have done. A simple word of appreciation can melt the rock of a man's heart.

After the awkward father-daughter hug was over, Patricia called the attention of her father as she was putting the milk in the refrigerator.

"Dad."

"Yes, my dear," Ray responded affectionately, still feeling elated from what transpired earlier.

"You know the percentages refer to fat and not water."

"Really? Well, the skim milk looked like 90% water."

Patricia chuckled.

"Seriously! I thought they skimmed the milk out of it and retained the water," Ray explained.

Patricia laughed uncontrollably.

Ray started being more involved in helping the older

children with their homework assignments too. The first thing that became quickly apparent to him was that the children needed to learn a lot. He felt the children do not know anything. To the contrary, the children behave as if they are scholars already. He started having more profound appreciation for teachers who teach these annoying kids in grade school.

"Truly, their *reward is in heaven* but a little bit in this world will be appreciated though," Ray mused to himself.

One thing was certain though, Ray got to know his children better through spending more time with them. Gradually, he warmed up to engaging them in conversations. Sometimes, he will defend a position he did not even share just to make his children reason and fight for their opinions.

One bright sunny Saturday afternoon, Lisa regretted, "I wish it is snowing."

"Interesting! Why would you want it to snow when we are in Summer?" Ray asked her.

"I am bored. I feel like going outside but it is hot. However, if we were in winter and pretty cold, we could have snow. In that case, I could go out and make an abominable snowman."

"Oh, I see." Ray remarked. Suddenly something sparked in his ears and he faced Lisa and asked, "would you have been making a bad, wicked snowman?"

Lisa chuckled and nodded in affirmation, not quite understanding what she was being asked.

Patricia then chimed in into the conversation uninvited and remarked, "Dad, she said abominable snowman because all snowmen are abominable."

"Really? What made them abominable?" Ray asked Patricia.

"I don't know, but people always say abominable snowman," Patricia replied.

"Would it be because it was made of snow or because it was a man?" Ray persisted.

"I don't know," Patricia reiterated.

"If we were to make a snowwoman, what would that be?" Ray inquired.

"Then, it would be an adorable snowwoman," Patricia responded.

"Oh, I see. Abominable is for the snowman but adorable is for the snowwoman, right?"

"Hmmm!" Patricia sighed.

"How early does the society make girls develop all these bad raps against boys and men?" Ray wondered to himself. He then turned to Patricia and asked, "Why is it that bad things are given masculine appellations?"

"Hmmm! Like what, dad?"

"It is old man winter because people don't like the cold." Patricia chuckled.

"If a woman kills somebody by mistake, they still call it manslaughter even though the crime was committed by a woman. They even blame men for their period by calling it menstruation too. Thereby, accusing men of causing that agonizing period for them."

"Hmmm! Well...." Patricia struggled with a response.

Ray continued. "It is pop quiz because students don't like them even if their teacher is a woman."

"I don't like pop quiz too, dad. Nobody likes them," Lisa expressed.

"Which part? The pop part or the quiz part?"

"The quiz part that pops from nowhere," Patricia replied laughing.

Ray decided to spend more time with the girls, so he suggested that they take a walk and Lisa can show him where she would have built her abominable snow man if they had two feet of snow. When Ray opened the front door, he noticed that Paige was standing next to his car. He looked closely and realized that it appeared that he was writing something. All of sudden, Paige looked up and saw that his dad was looking at him from the porch in front of the house with Lisa and Patricia by his side.

Paige stopped what he was doing and ran away from the driveway. As he was running on the grass that he cut earlier that morning before the weather became hot, Ray called him.

"Paige! Paige! Come back here!" Ray shouted.

Paige stopped running and started walking back slowly

towards his father who had started making his way to the driver side of his car where Paige was standing before he took to his heels.

Ray chuckled. "I see. My car was talking to you."

Patricia and Lisa were laughing uncontrollably when they saw what Paige had written on daddy's car.

"Shut up! It is not funny," Paige shouted at his sisters.

"Shut down! We did not think it is funny too. It is incredibly hilarious!" Patricia replied as she and Lisa laughed louder knowing fully well that Paige is in big trouble.

Ray looked at Paige trying not to show his feeling and maintained his composure. "He turned and faced Paige again. "Let me get this straight. You were cutting the grass earlier this morning. My car was looking at you and it developed a friendship bond with you. So, it decided to send its telepathic message to the rest of the world through you. Is that what happened here?"

Paige lowered his head but kept quiet. However, he noted that his father was not raising his voice at all. That cold, flat tone of his father's voice was what was bothering him the most. He expected him to be shouting at him at the minimum. Rather, his father was speaking to him as if he was just a non-judgmental investigator who was only trying to ascertain facts.

"Mr Car Language Translator, can you please ask my car if it is hungry too since you understand its language?"

Paige chuckled. Now he felt a sense of awkward relief that his father is going to be lenient with him.

"Yeah! Can you ask it if its tires hurt?" Patricia chimed in making fun of Paige.

"Shut up!" Paige replied her.

"Shut down!" Patricia replied him. "What were you thinking?"

Paige was silent.

"There is no problem here," Ray commented. He turned and faced Paige "go ahead and carry out the wishes of your car buddy here."

"I er er er...don't know what you mean." Paige mumbled.

"C'mon Paige. My car sent you a telepathic distress call which you promptly wrote on it, right?" Ray asked him rhetorically.

Hmmm! Paige sighed.

"What my car told you in car language is what you wrote in English language, right?"

Paige was silent.

"Ok. Read what you wrote!" Ray instructed Paige.

"Wash me. Please!" Paige responded.

"It is a simple request. So, go on and carry it out. Wash the car."

"B..b..but I have not washed a car before."

"That is my fault which the car was trying to correct. You are fourteen years old now. In less than two years, you will be writing *'drive me please'* on my car in an attempt to convince me to let you drive my car. Worse still, you may be hoping to get your own car too. No doubt, you really need training on car etiquettes. So, the car wants you to start with knowing how to take care of a car by hand washing it."

Paige sighed.

Patricia and Lisa started laughing again.

"Just get a bucket. The car wash detergent and car towel are on the shelf in the garage. You already have water in the water hose for watering the lawn. Simply detach the fountain head and you have your water supply."

"Hmmm!" Paige sighed again.

"Congratulations! Welcome to your first car wash. I trust you will make the car proud," Ray chuckled as he pat Paige on his left shoulder. "In less than 2 years, the car will probably talk to you saying, *'drive me please.'*" Ray made air quotes on saying drive me please.

Paige sighed again with disappointment written on his face.

Ray turned to Paige and offered his hand to Paige, which he took rather reluctantly.

"Thank you very much my beloved son," Ray expressed while giving Paige a firm handshake. "I don't know how I forgot that boys could wash cars using just a towel and a bucket. It was what we did as kids. I do apologize to your generation. We have not trained our boys well."

He then left with his daughters to take a stroll in the neighborhood. They went for a short walk discussing different topics that the girls were interested in. Ray was not interested in most of what they talked about, but he listened to his girls talk and just chimed in from time to time. For Lisa, it was an enjoyable walk because on their way back, they saw an ice-cream truck and Ray bought ice cream for them.

As the fourth of July independence holiday drew near, Ray was watching television with his children when a commercial came on for "independence holiday furniture sale." This jolted Bryan's memory of watching the beautiful Independence Day fireworks display on television.

"I think it would be a lot of fun if we could have our own firework display in the yard," Bryan commented.

"Bad idea," Paige responded.

"Why?" Bryan asked him.

"Dad told me before that it is a major fire hazard. It is also illegal."

Bryan turned to Ray and asked "Dad, is that true?"

"Yes. Moreover, it is a waste of money."

"How?" Bryan asked with disappointment in his voice.

"Let us assume you bought few fireworks for twenty dollars," Ray continued.

"Yes, dad."

"Then, you light a matchstick and set fire to the fireworks. It will go up into the sky and display beautiful colors or it may simply explode making a loud noise that will thrill the people around, right?"

"Yes, dad."

"That is the end. In a few seconds of short-lived colors and a loud noise, your twenty dollars is gone. That is it!"

"Hmmm!" Bryan grumbled.

"The fact is that the government puts up a show of fireworks on the National Mall in Washington DC on our behalf using our taxes. It costs about three hundred thousand dollars for about thirty minutes of colorful display."

"Hmmm!" Bryan sighed trying to resign to fate.

"Dad"

"Yes, Paige"

"Can we go and watch the display on the National Mall?"

"Hmmm!" Ray sighed. "The mall is usually crowded. However, we can get close enough to see the fireworks but still be reasonably far enough to avoid the rowdiness at the mall."

"Awesome! Thanks dad. You are the best," Paige responded in excitement.

In the early evening of July fourth, Ray, Patricia, Paige, Bryan and Lisa left to watch the Independence Day fireworks. Desiree and Amanda stayed at home. They found a great spot on Mount Vernon Trail after sunset and got a fantastic view in the direction of the National Mall.

While waiting for the fireworks display to start, Ray engaged his children in history lessons.

"Lisa, what do you think the Independence Day celebration was for?"

"I em..em.." Lisa tried to search her mind for the answer.

"I think it was when the slaves were freed. They got their independence, right?" Bryan suggested.

"Oh no!" Paige responded. "It was the United States that declared her independence from the British."

"Excellent! However, it seems you guys need a lot of history lessons," Ray concluded. "The Emancipation Day or Juneteenth was when slaves were declared freed in Texas on June 19, 1865."

"It was great to go and see the Liberty Bell in Philadelphia. Can we go to other places?" Patricia inquired.

"That is a good idea. I have a vacation coming up for ten days about three weeks from now. Maybe we can make something happen in that period."

"That would be really awesome!" Patricia opined.

"What historical places or places of interest would you want us to go?" Ray asked his children.

"We can start with where the people arrived in the country," Patricia suggested.

"The airport?" Bryan asked.

"C'mon! The first permanent English colony was established by settlers who arrived at Jamestown in Virginia a long time ago," Patricia responded.

"Okay. We can start our history journey from there. Any other places on your radar?" Ray inquired.

"I want to see the statue of liberty," Paige responded.

"That is in New York," Patricia reminded him.

"Yes. I know. It is supposed to be on an island somewhere there," Paige replied.

All the children looked at Ray for his answer, but their eyes said it all. They wanted a *"YES"* answer. They have never been to New York and they would love to go.

"Do you guys want to go to New York?" Ray asked rhetorically.

"Yes!" They shouted almost in unison.

"I will think about it and discuss with your mum."

Suddenly, the rapid whistling sound and exploding colorful display of the Independence Day fireworks lit the evening sky. It was beautiful.

"Wow!" Lisa exclaimed.

"Awesome!" Bryan shouted.

About forty minutes later, they started packing their things to leave for home after the fireworks display. Ray then commented, "this is my point. If daddy paid for this thirty-minutes show, it would have cost him a lot more than his salary for an entire year."

Ray discussed with Desiree about taking the children on the road trip. They will go to Jamestown and return home the same day. Then, they will head for New York two days later to spend two nights in New York City and complete the trip by catching a view of the Niagara Falls before heading home. Desiree agreed with the trip, but she will only go with them to Jamestown. She did not want to go with them to New York with Amanda.

The trip to Jamestown was quite uneventful. It was an enlightening experience.

**Travel on earth through air, land or water and
discover the world beyond your nose.**

In Jamestown, they learnt about the history of the settlers
and the settlement from the guides who were dressed in the
attires simulating the dress patterns of the settlers of the old.
They were given information about the challenges faced by the
settlers, their community organization, and the all-important
interactions with the native American tribe in the area.

After returning home, Ray rented a Honda Odyssey
minivan for the trip to New York City and Niagara Falls
even though he was not looking forward to an odyssey.
However, traveling by road, by himself, for four days with
his four children will always be a recipe for an odyssey.

Ray decided to give his children a special treat the night
before the trip at the dinner table.

"If you guys get ready early enough tomorrow morning
that I do not have to wait for you and we are able to beat the
rush hour traffic, I am thinking of making a detour
somewhere on our way to a place that will surprise you."

"Excellent! Dad, where?" Patricia asked.

"It is a surprise reward only if you guys are on time
tomorrow."

"Mum, where is the surprise place dad is planning to take us tomorrow?" Patricia faced Desiree.

Desiree smiled while shaking her head at the game Patricia was playing. She tapped Patricia on her left shoulder and remarked, "your dad is still sitting here, you can ask him directly yourself."

"Hmmm!" Patricia sighed and then put on a fake smile. "Dad, assuming we are early tomorrow as you wanted, where are you going to take us for our surprise treat?"

"All I can tell you is that if you are ready on time, you will see the surprise place when we get there tomorrow. However, if you are late by one minute, we are only going to drive straight to New York."

"The place must be between here and New York," Paige opined.

"Obviously," Patricia commented while looking at Ray's face hoping to get a clue about the surprise place, but he just ignored her.

"Dad, how far is the surprise place from here?" Patricia asked undeterred.

"A few hours if there is no traffic congestion."

Patricia resigned to fate. She became convinced that she would not be able to pry the information about the surprise place out of Ray.

"What time are we leaving tomorrow so that we can go to the surprise place?" Patricia inquired.

"All of you have to be fully packed and be seated in the car by 0600 hours military time!" Ray stated while trying to sound like a drill sergeant.

Paige looked at Patricia and remarked "isn't that 6 o'clock in the morning?"

"Y-y-yes?" Patricia replied him wondering why he needed to ask when it was so obvious.

"That is so early!" Paige commented.

"It is not too early dad." Patricia spoke to Ray with reassurance. She then looked at her siblings and spoke with authority. "We are making that 6 o'clock time guys. We need to get that surprise from dad. Sleep in the car when he drives if you like, but you are all waking up early. We are all packing tonight, you can take shower tonight before you go to bed if you want."

Ray leaned over to Desiree and whispered something in her left ear. She giggled and slapped him lovingly on his right hand.

"What?" Patricia asked, looking at her parents, but directing the question to no one in particular.

Ray and Desiree shrugged their shoulders in unison, but they did not say anything.

Patricia got up and said to her siblings. "Finish your food quickly. Go upstairs and start packing."

Within a few minutes, the children were all done with their food and left Ray and Desiree at the dining table.

In the morning, Ray was woken up by some noise in the hallway. He looked at the clock, it was 5:05 in the morning. He got up from the bed and slightly opened their bedroom door. He peeped through the door and saw that Lisa was dragging a traveling bag. He wondered when the children woke up. He yawned and stretched as if trying to increase his wingspan by a foot. Desiree opened her eyes.

"Well, you said so yourself. She is a fiery leader that sounded like a little me." Desiree commented as she turned to her left side to continue her sleep.

Ray simply shook his head. He must hurry up himself not to be late to the vehicle for their journey. He quickly made his way into the bathroom to get ready.

Desiree had packed a lot of 'survival items' for Ray in this father-children bonding expedition. She packed a lot of snacks, juice, water, baked foods, and many microwavable delicacies.

Ray referred to his children as his 'co-land pilots' on the trip. They ate breakfast items of different combinations of cold cereal, croissant, bread, peanut butter and cream cheese spread. Ray pulled out of the driveway onto the road at exactly 6.05 am for their trip.

"Dad."

"Yes"

"Now that we made it on time…"

"Yes."

"Where are we going for the surprise?" Patricia finally asked her question, still curious about the surprise stopover her dad promised them.

"Good job to all of you. Since you guys made it on time, I am going to fulfill my promise to you. That is why we are going to......... where we are going."

"Hmmm!" Patricia grumbled. For a moment, she thought that her father was planning to tell them where they were going before heading to New York.

Within thirty minutes of the trip, all the children were fast asleep.

"Are we there yet?" Lisa asked about an hour and half later when she spontaneously opened her eyes.

"Almost," Ray responded.

Lisa went back to sleep.

About an hour later, Ray pulled into the parking lot.

Patricia opened her eyes and shook her head. Her eyes brightened immediately.

"Hersheypark!" She shouted waking Paige and Lisa up in the process. Bryan remained asleep and Paige nudged him to wake up that daddy brought them to Hersheypark as the surprise.

"But dad, Hershey is not directly on the way to New York. When we Googled 'interesting places of interest between Maryland and New York,' Hershey did not come up," Patricia commented as if trying to justify why they did not have any idea where Ray planned to take them for the surprise.

"Yes, you are correct. However, I said that we will make a detour to a place that will surprise you," Ray reminded her. "We have roughly one hour to visit Hershey's Chocolate World and go on the chocolate tour. Afterwards, we will go into Hersheypark for the rides, but you only have a few hours before we head to New York. I don't want to arrive late to New York as I want us to go to Times Square tonight if possible."

"Excellent!" Paige remarked as they made their way into the chocolate world.

The children had a lot of fun reading the information on

the wall regarding the history of Hershey's chocolate. The educational tour of how the chocolates were made was very enlightening for all of them including Ray. The environment was beautiful. The smell of chocolate filled the air. After the tour, they were given free samples of Hershey's kisses chocolate. Ray bought some chocolates in the store as well.

Swing, chill and enjoy the thrill.

They experienced *'Hersheypark Happy'* starting with measuring their heights to ascertain what rides they could go on. They went on some initial simple swings as they walked into the theme park. Later, Ray joined his children on a ride called *The Claw*, a swinging pendulum which scared Ray and made him dizzy. He settled for *Livery Stables*, a low-speed ride on plastic horses. Ray did not bother to join the children for any more rides, and he spared himself the embarrassment of crying or vomiting on a roller coaster. His children, however, had a lot of fun enjoying gravity defying rides and roller coasters with funny names. Their major regret was that they had to leave after a few hours in order to get to New York in a reasonable time.

**These slowly moving horses in *Livery Stables* are not
competing in the Kentucky Derby.**

The drive to New York from Hershey to New York was
exciting to the children as they could not stop reliving their
wonderful experience at the theme park. They talked and
argued about which ride was the scariest. Ray could not
weigh in the conversation since he did not go on any roller
coaster.

"Dad"

"Yes"

"Why were you screaming on *The Claw*?" Patricia asked
her dad with tongue in cheek.

"I didn't find it funny at all. When the pendulum was
swinging towards the ground, I felt as if it was going to crash
on the ground."

"I wasn't scared," Paige remarked.

"Good for you," Ray responded.

"You should have come on *The Fahrenheit* dad. It was a
very scary roller coaster," Patricia lamented. *The Claw* was
not even scary at all.

"Okay my lovely brave children! Thank you for your
counseling. I will keep it in mind for next time that is not coming."

"I didn't know that you get scared that easily dad," Patricia rubbed it in.

"Patsy!" Ray called Patricia as he typically calls her when he is fond of her.

"Yes dad."

"When we get to the next rest stop, remind me to give you up for adoption to the first stranger we see."

"That is not going to happen dad."

"And why is that?"

"Because you will miss me too much."

"No, we won't!" Bryan chimed in eagerly.

"Keep quiet. Nobody is talking to you," Patricia snarled at Bryan.

"Exactly why we won't miss you," Bryan replied.

"Dad, I know you are going to miss me. I am sure that you are going to cry more than mum when I get married."

"Don't hold your breath on that!" Ray responded.

"Hmmm! I know what I know dad."

"Okay! You are right, but I am only going to miss you a tiny bit," Ray agreed while demonstrating how little he is going to miss Patricia using a hardly noticeable space between his right index finger and his thumb.

Four hours of driving later, they finally arrived in the parking lot of their hotel in New York City after surviving the grueling traffic congestion in New York City's Lincoln Tunnel for about an hour. After checking into their hotel, they had a dinner buffet in a restaurant in the hotel and headed to Times Square which was only a few blocks from their hotel. It was a spectacular scene with all the neon lights. They walked around a bit enjoying the scenery. They got some souvenirs of New York City including key chains, tee shirts, purses, and hats.

"We need to head back to the hotel so that you can rest. Tomorrow is bound to be a long day," Ray informed his children.

Reluctantly, they went back to the hotel. Ray had booked two hotel rooms in New York Downtown for two days and another two hotel rooms for a night in close proximity to Niagara Falls on the American side of the Falls for their trip.

Time moves slowly in Times Square

"Dad"

"Yes, Bryan"

"Can we stay longer in New York?" Bryan asked him as they were getting on the elevator in their hotel suite.

"No, but why?"

"I would like to see more places in New York."

"I am sorry," Ray sympathized.

"B-b-but Dad, if we stay a week more, we will pay less."

"What makes you think that we will pay less if we stay longer?" Ray asked him.

"A sign in the hotel lobby stated that *Stay More, Pay Less.*"

"Really?"

"Yes dad."

"Sorry Bryan. They are trying to game us with numbers, we will always pay more the longer we stay." Ray tried to explain. "Okay, let us do the mathematics. If we stay for two days at $200 per day, we will pay $400. If we chose to stay for 7 days, the price drops to $180 per day so that instead of paying $1400, we will pay $1,260. We still end up paying more money, but the rate is what reduces. It is just a marketing gimmick trying to get us to spend more money by staying longer."

The following morning, they woke up early and had complimentary breakfast in the hotel lobby. They subsequently took the New York City Subway transit to the departure depot to board their ferry to Ellis Island and the Statue of Liberty. The trip was very enlightening. They learnt about the history of Ellis Island and the role it played in processing immigrants to the United States in the recent past. The ferry ride took them around the magnificent edifice *Liberty Enlightening the World* also known as The Statue of Liberty. It was a colossal structure that is well recognized throughout the world as a symbol of freedom.

Bring me your exhausted poor people with hope in their hearts...... for me to set them free!

The plan made by Ray for all the places he wanted the children to visit had a major flaw with the plan; he did not account for New York traffic and mass transit challenges in his plan. Time was not on their side. Ray had planned for them to go to the Bronx Zoo and the Brooklyn Botanical Garden as well.

Zoom into the zoo for the wild have been brought nearer.

By the time they got off the bus and made it to the gate of the zoo, it was about to close for the day. Therefore, they quickly made their way using connecting bus services to the botanical garden. Unfortunately, local traffic was not co-operative as well and they arrived just twenty minutes before the closing time. The attendant suggested for them to come back another day as it would not be optimal educational experience for the children if they could only spend a few minutes in the botanical garden. Thus, they did not see the animals of the zoo and they did not observe the beautiful flowers and exotic plants they were yearning to see in the botanical garden.

The garden of beautiful flowers and exotic plants

Therefore, they got back on the mass transit bus to explore *The Central Park* instead before it was too dark.

The following day, they checked out of the hotel after breakfast and headed to Niagara Falls. Ray got food from a drive through and they ate in the car before they reached Niagara Falls. When they reached their hotel in the evening, they went straight to bed after checking into the hotel. Although they were tired, they were excited about visiting the waterfalls the following day.

Niagara Falls.....where gallons of water fall before your eyes

After breakfast, they took a short nap and then checked out of the hotel to head to the waterfalls. One of the attendants at the hotel mentioned to Ray that the view of the waterfalls is better on the Canadian side. Ray and his children could not verify this claim because they did not come with their United States passports and could not cross the border into Canada. The view of the waterfalls was spectacular. The site of the body of water was astonishing. The splashing water in the bright sunlight created a rainbow in the waterfall. There were lots of people at the three waterfalls. They noticed people on a ferry in the water itself. The children became curious and wanted to take the ferry ride too, but Ray refused. They took a lot of pictures and got some snacks at the restaurant on site at the waterfalls. Then they headed for their car to go back home.

If you chase waterfalls, do not fall with it.

When they left Niagara Falls around noon, they stopped by a diner and ate. A couple of hours later, Paige broke the silence in the car as they drove through a town.

"Dad."

"Yes"

"Ice cream will be so awesome right now."

"Interesting suggestion," Ray commented with an understanding that the children are just trying to be mischievous. "Well, they got it from their mother," Ray said to himself.

Suddenly, Bryan shouted, "Daddy! Look at the sign board over there."

"Yes. I could see the sign for the Laundromat," Ray replied.

"Not the laundromat dad, but above it," Patricia chimed in.

"Yes. I see it now. I can see the *Destiny Manicure and Pedicure* sign."

"Above that dad. It is *Snow Terry Ice Cream* sign," Paige responded.

"Oh my, we just passed it," Ray regretted with tongue in cheek.

"But we can turn back dad," Bryan suggested.

"Going backward is not good for anyone, right? So, let us keep going forward."

All the children grumbled together.

They arrived at home in the evening after driving for about nine hours. They were all exhausted.

After Desiree finished her Master of Business Administration degree, she got a job as Marketing Manager in a Fortune 500 Company in the District of Columbia. The pay was good, but the demands of the job was high. Desiree had decreasing time to spend at home with her family. Patricia and Paige watch over Bryan and Lisa when they get back from school. Ray continued to complain that what he needed in his life is a wife and not a Marketing Manager. Desiree ignored his comment saying to herself that she had worked too hard to get to where she was and she would not want to lose her opportunity.

One evening after picking Amanda late from her daycare center, Desiree overhead a conversation between Paige and Patricia. Her two older children were arguing over an issue that Desiree could not determine when Patricia remarked, "I would advise you not to put any of your eggs in mummy's basket. She is a corporate lady who has no time for her children."

The statement struck Desiree like a lightning bolt. She recalled that it was Patricia who had commented previously that her dad was the star of the house because he is the one who was working. Her statement back then did not reflect someone who appreciated her mum's efforts in raising them when she was a homemaker. Nonetheless, the comment bothered Desiree tremendously. The following day, she called Susan and related her challenges to her.

"Try and spend some time with them. You can take them out for ice cream and the like but buy them gifts of the latest electronic gadgets that these teenagers love. Afterall, you don't need to ask Ray for the money anymore," Susan suggested.

"That is true. I can take them on an outing in my new Nissan Pathfinder over the weekend," Desiree agreed.

"Nice ride, isn't it?"

"It is elegant," Desiree asserted.

"Ha ha! It was as if you were sending a message that you are finding your own path. You go girl!"

"Thanks, but Ray keeps complaining more and more."

"Don't mind him. He is just having a tough time adjusting to your new status. Maybe, he is just one of those men who cannot handle being with successful wives."

"Hmmm!" Desiree sighed. "The comment of Patricia bothers me though. Am I failing as a mother?"

"I don't think so. Look at it this way. When you help pay for her college, she will be glad she has you as her mother. Whatever sentiments she has now will disappear and she will be filled with profound gratitude."

The following Saturday, Desiree went to attend an all-day workshop organized by her company. She left home very early as the workshop was scheduled to start at 8 o'clock in the morning and end at 5 o'clock in the afternoon.

At about noon, Ray was in the kitchen with Patricia. Both of them were doing house chores unwillingly.

"I don't understand this dad," Patricia complained.

"Understand what?"

"You told us not to waste resources but that is precisely what you are making me do here."

"What did you mean?"

"Okay dad. We have a dishwasher here that is sitting idle and it is not doing anything in particular. Yet, you insisted that I wash these plates in the kitchen sink by hand using the dishwashing soap. Isn't that wasting of precious resources through underutilization of the dishwasher?"

Ray chuckled. "You are right, but the more precious resources that will be wasted will be your brain and your hands if they are not put to adequate use. That's is why I am trying to make you use those ones rather than dishwasher which is just mechanical."

"Hmmm!" Patricia grumbled and frowned temporarily. However, she wasn't going to give up. If she failed in avoiding washing plates now, she may succeed later. After all, washing plates now, will also mean washing plates later. Hopefully, dad will finally figure out how to cook the special dish he is trying to replicate by watching a YouTube video.

"Dad, you know that we can simply order Chinese food. Those guys will bring disposable plates as well. You don't need to cook the recipe you are watching on YouTube and I don't have to wash plates, That sounds like a great win-win situation for both of us, right?"

"I am not learning how to cook by watching a video, I just wanted to see the style of this chef," Ray replied defensively.

"Well, all I am saying is that we can solve our problems together. In thirty minutes, the food can be delivered by Wonton Chow and there will be no uncertainty in taste."

Ray paused for a moment. "On second thought, I think I am going to agree with you." Ray commented. He had vegetable oil in his right hand and the frying pan in his left hand. He put them down and addressed Patricia directly.

"I think you should quickly go upstairs to your room. Look under your bed and bring your piggy bank on which you wrote *Bank of Maryland*. Bring it so that we can take the money out of it and order food as you recommended. I will order Chinese for you and Paige, Japanese for me, Vietnamese for Bryan and Lebanese for Lisa."

Patricia stood motionless in shock. She was surprised with her dad's answer. She did not know that Ray knew that her piggy bank was under her bed. She was dumbfounded. However, she did not move. One thing was certain though, she wasn't going to use her hard-earned money that she has been saving for a long time to buy food for anybody. Her plan was straightforward. She plans to buy herself a

Cinderella-type maxi dress and shoes. Well, dad's cooking is not going to kill them. It may even miraculously turn out to be delicious.

She looked at her dad and smiled shaking her head. Ray smiled back. His point was well understood by his daughter.

Ray poured some vegetable oil into the frying pan as instructed in the video and put the pot on the cooker to replicate the sauce he just watched on YouTube.

Suddenly, there was a loud cry from Lisa in the living room. Ray and Patricia left the kitchen and rushed to the living room to see the emergency that was going on there. When they got to the living room, they found Lisa sitting on the floor on the carpet moving her arms in air and shaking her legs vigorously while crying loudly. Ray quickly rushed to her and lifted her up trying to figure out what happened to her. Bryan was sitting quietly in the corner of the sofa across from Lisa. The whole scene appeared bizarre and Ray could not make out what was going on. At that moment Paige started walking away.

"And where are you going young man?" Ray faced him while pulling Lisa to her feet.

"To the bathroom," Paige replied.

"What did you do to her?" Ray asked him with anger in his voice.

"I didn't do anything to her. It was Bryan that was making faces at her."

"That is why she shouted like that and was crying as if a calamity has befallen her?" Ray inquired being unsure of the answer he got.

Paige simply shrugged his shoulders as he walked away.

Ray turned to Lisa and moved her chin up to look at her face. "Is that true?"

"Y-y-yes" Lisa mumbled.

Ray could not believe his ears and he shouted, "You are crying that loudly because he made faces at you?"

But before Lisa could respond, the smoke alarm in the kitchen went off screaming another emergency. Ray quickly left the children in the living room and headed straight to the kitchen. There was an intense smoke from the oil that has overheated in the frying pan. The smoke alarm continued its annoying doomsday noise. Ray instructed Patricia to open all the windows for the smoke to dissipate. He took the frying pan off the cooker and switched it off. In the heat of the moment, he did not know what to do. The whole atmosphere was chaotic. There were other pots on the cooker. One of the pots was being used to cook basmati white rice. He put the frying pan on the floor where he was standing while trying to gather his thoughts. He quickly used the newspaper in the breakfast area of the kitchen to blow air across the smoke alarm to increase the chances of ending the shriek noise it was making. The smoke alarm noise stopped suddenly bringing some relief to the chaotic scene. Ray took the frying pan from the floor and immediately realized the mistake he had made. The hot frying pan had burnt the carpet making the shape of the bottom of the frying pan on the carpet.

It has been overwhelming for him to be dealing with the children. They don't know anything. They cry for nothing. They dirty the whole house and yet, they protest when you tell them to clean it up. It was as if they had no idea that they are not the only ones in the world.

All he could think of was to give all of them time out to face different corners of the walls and have them glued there until lunch is ready so that he would not have to put up with their mischief, but he knew that he could not do it. They are too old for that.

Patricia called Ray's attention to the carpet and he replied that he had seen it. Ray subsequently used another frying pan and cooked the recipe he watched on YouTube. The food was sumptuous. Patricia told her siblings about the burnt carpet and showed them when they came to eat.

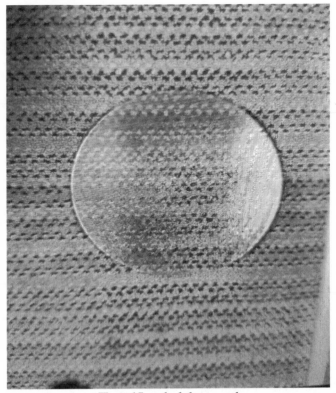

Honey! I cooked the carpet!

"We won't tell mummy about it," Ray suggested as they sat for lunch. He really wished Desiree will get her priorities right and be home to raise her children. He was sure that she would have known what to do with these children that were driving him crazy.

Anyone who follows good instructions can cook!

When Desiree arrived at home, Lisa met her at the door. After hugging her mum, she said, "daddy cooked very delicious food and burnt the carpet."

Desiree was puzzled with what she heard. She did not know what was more plausible. Was it Ray cooking delicious food or his burning the carpet?

While Desiree was trying to process wat she was told, Lisa held her hand and dragged her to the kitchen to show her the burnt carpet. When she saw the carpet, she shook her head but the aroma of the food in the kitchen caught her attention and she opened the pot. She was stunned to see the sauce prepared by Ray. She took a spoon to taste it and her taste buds busted into a symphony of exotic celebrations. She quickly took a plate and served herself some basmati rice. She served the delicious sauce over the rice. When she finished eating, she went into the bedroom and saw Ray who was taking off his shirt to take a nap.

"That food was delicious. You need to do more house chores. You also need to cook like this more often if you want to dance with me all night long," Desiree remarked.

Ray could not believe his ears. Did Desiree just tell him that he has to be doing housework if he wants to be with her. This was humiliation of the highest order. So, intimacy is now going to be a reward to him for being a "good boy" rather than his right? What an insult! Ray shook his head and responded, "you are a very ungrateful woman."

He put his shirt back on with severe anger written on his face. He left the bedroom and left the house to cool down. After walking for some time, he decided to give Mama Wise a call.

The following day, Desiree knocked on Mama Wise's door. Although she reluctantly agreed to come and meet with her, she was ready for this conversation. She reassured herself that the Desiree that was coming for this discussion was not the housewife that came to her a few years earlier, but a successful lady who is no longer a doormat for her husband.

After the initial exchange of pleasantries, Desiree and Mama Wise got into the heat of their discussion. The conversation quickly became turbulent and very antagonistic.

"I know that you may not see things from my perspectives, but there is no light at the end of the tunnel you are driving your marriage into. Your husband is missing you and your children are growing up without your loving presence," Mama Wise tried to jolt Desiree into reality.

"As per Ray, he needs to get over the idea that he married a housewife. As per my children, they know that I love them, and I care about them. I am doing all these for them anyway," Desiree replied with a touch of veiled anger in her voice.

"Really? Are you are doing these for them or for yourself?

C'mon my daughter! How is your not being there for them as their mother .....be that you are doing it for them?" Mama Wise asked rhetorically.

"I appreciate your concern, but I know what I am doing," Desiree gave a muted response.

"I actually sympathize with Ray, but I am fearful for you."

"Why?"

"You are denying your husband something that you really don't want him to go and get elsewhere. You are playing a bad game using a strategy that will only work temporarily until your husband throws his hands up in the air. He will soon say to himself that he is a grown man and can make his decisions even if they are inimical to your interests. If you let it happen, you would have succeeded in setting your marriage on fire with your own hands."

"You sound like a domesticated woman. No pun intended! As women, we have our rights and desires too. We need to claim our equality to our husbands. We shouldn't be subservient to them. There should not be a big deal with him spending more time with his children. After all, they are his children too. I didn't produce them all alone, right?"

"This is only about understanding how marriage works my dear. Imagine that your husband fights back withholding paying rent, withholding house maintenance allowance, his children's school fees and he said he will not do any of them if he is not getting his due time with you. How will that make you feel?"

"With all due respect mam, but you really sound like a subjugated woman. If anything, I hope he is smart enough not to do that,"

"And who is going to stop him? You?"

"No problem if he is stupid enough to do what you said. I don't depend on him anymore anyway. I have a very good job and I am financially stable. He will be asked to pay child support on his children."

"Just listen to yourself. We are talking about a man who is taking care of his responsibilities. What he is spending on you and his children right now will always be more than whatever you will get from him as child support. Moreover, if he leaves you, your children will absolutely lack the father who loves them and is committed to them. Now, that has no price tag. It is priceless. Wake up Desiree!"

"Your talking this way has only convinced me more that I made the right decision to pursue my career path and be financially independent. Enough of being a doormat. I am an independent woman. I am free to make my own decisions."

"You really have no appreciation for the good husband that you have. What gave you the impression that there are many men out there that are better than your husband? Moreover, what gave you the assurance that they will be interested in you?"

Desiree chuckled in embarrassment

"Well, I can see that you are a very beautiful woman, but don't think that at almost 40 years of age, a lot of men will be picking numbers to knock on your door after having five children."

"Excuse me! I don't need any man in my life. I can take care of my children."

"My dear, every married couple always have 'issues.' Mama Wise reassured Desiree making air quotes while saying *issues*. If any couple tells you that they don't have issues, you should just know that they have just told you that they have telling lies as an additional issue too."

Desiree smiled, but remained quiet.

"Hmmm! How things have changed and remained the same at the same time. You were focusing on your children and neglecting your husband previously. Now, you are neglecting your husband and your children. Nevertheless, a few minutes ago, you stated that you are only concerned about your children."

"Ray is a grown-up. He should be able to take care of himself."

"Remember that if you choose your children over your husband, your children will eventually leave the nest. You will not have a true loving husband to be stuck with when your nest becomes empty. I am just advising you from the vantage point of view of an imperfect wife and mother who raised six children and happened to have been married to two husbands at different points in her life."

"Hmmm!" Desiree sighed.

"Don't focus too much on your children or your career to the detriment of your marriage. The only children that stick around are the disabled ones. Nobody prays to have disabled children. You don't have to be a genius to know that there will be no meeting point to resolve your differences with your husband if you are not doing your responsibilities in your home. I know you don't really see it because of your befogged mind regarding whatever it is that you are pursuing. However, you actually have a wonderful husband that most women will kill for. Your husband is a successful lawyer in a high place. He has a good career and is financially stable. He clearly loves you and he doesn't cheat on you."

"And how did you know that?" Desiree inquired with doubt in her voice.

"If your husband is cheating on you, he will not be very angry with you and get destabilized every time you pummel him with '*No! Leave me alone.*' You don't seem to get it. If he had been cheating on you, he would have gone to satisfy himself outside and will have nothing left in his tank for you at all. He probably will even stop asking you on a regular basis because he will be on a prowl for a much younger blood. You have to understand that only able-bodied, committed men ask all the time and get very angry when denied because they are not thinking of alternatives. Don't be stupid and open the door of alternatives for your husband."

"You seemed to be condoning such a behavior."

"Not at all. I am only trying to make you see the implications of what you are doing. If you frustrate your husband and you push him to reach a breaking point, you will lose him. Think about it for a second. You want to lose a good husband because of an activity that will take less than twenty minutes of your time. You may end up with a lifetime of regrets and you may never be able to fix the problem. Don't lose him before you appreciate him."

Desiree got upset and stood up abruptly to leave.

"Desiree, I hope you find whatever you are looking for. I sincerely hope you find it quickly too and its worth is more than what you are giving up for it. As far as I am concerned, you are putting yourself on the path of losing a good loving husband."

"Don't tell me how I should run my life," Desiree snarled.

"I am not telling you how to run your life, I am merely advising you not to ruin it."

"Yours is the backward generation that allowed men to trample upon you as they like. In my generation, we will not put up with such nonsense."

"Maybe the better analysis you should do is to ask yourself about the endpoint. Whatever you think your 'sophisticated' generation has accomplished, has it made you happier than our 'stupid' generation as you referred to us?' Mama Wise asked while raising her voice and making air quotes when she said *sophisticated* and *stupid*. "Yeah! Go ahead and confirm to yourself that your 'liberated' generation is happier than our 'subjugated' generation," Mama Wise chided Desiree while making air quotes on saying *liberated* and *subjugated*.

Her response made Desiree pause for a moment.

Mama Wise was clearly upset, and she continued to talk even as Desiree started going towards the door to leave unceremoniously. "Are you really going to be happy if your responsible and loving husband gets completely frustrated into leaving you because you were pursuing a career and you neglected your responsibilities to your family?"

Desiree knew that happiness is always the goal that we all strive for, but she had never put things in perspectives to address happiness as an end point of her issues. However, that was not the time for such analysis. That was not the time. She gently closed the door of Mama Wise's apartment and headed for the stairs.

About a month later, Ray was pacing back and forth in

the living room waiting for Desiree to get dressed for them to leave for Germantown for Desiree's cousin's wedding. The wedding supposed to start at noon. Ray looked at his watch for the umpteenth time. It read 11:10 AM. He had been waiting for her for fifteen minutes already. He was fast running out of patience.

"You are going to make us get there late!" Ray yelled as he started climbing the stairs to go back to the bedroom to hurry Desiree up.

"I am almost done," Desiree responded.

Ray busted through the bedroom door. His mouth became ajar in disbelief. He found Desiree standing in front of the mirror holding a red dress in her right hand and a blue dress in her left hand. She was wearing only her white camisole and leggings.

"You have not even dressed up!" Ray yelled at her and he continued to complain about how insensitive she was about time.

Desiree ignored his tirade. Rather, she turned to him and asked, "should I wear this red dress or this blue dress?"

Her nonchalant attitude about her timing was unbearable for Ray. Although he was quite frustrated, he was not in the mood for any unpleasant drama. Therefore, instead of addressing her question, Ray started undressing.

"Baby, we really don't need to go anywhere," Ray addressed Desiree while removing his tie. "You know what, don't wear anything. I actually prefer you not to wear anything. Let us just keep each other company in this our special space, in this special place in this our special room."

"What!" Desiree exclaimed.

Ray was undeterred as he moved closer to Desiree trying to hug her as he started to undo the buttons of his shirt.

"Anyway, we can always apologize to your cousin. We have already picked and paid for a gift for them at their registry. In any case, they won't miss us," Ray concluded.

He approached her and held her hands. Desiree snatched her hands from him. She took her clothes straight to the bathroom attached to the master's bedroom and locked the door. Thirty seconds later, she was fully dressed in her blue dress and was standing by the bedroom door for them to leave.

Ray had taken off his shirt. He started insisting that they should stay at home and celebrate on behalf of Desiree's cousin 'in their own way.' He proceeded towards Desiree trying to kiss her. Desiree quickly left the bedroom and continued her brisk walk downstairs while telling Ray that they needed to leave. Reluctantly, Ray put his shirt back on and put on his tie. When they got to the door of the house, they noticed the sky was dark and there was a heavy downpour of rain. Therefore, they ran into the car. There was a flash of lightning followed by a deafening thunder as they entered their vehicle.

After a few minutes of awkward silence in the car, Desiree started reflecting on her continued struggles as she juggles her family responsibilities with her job demands. Childcare service for Amanda has been getting more and more challenging given her long work hours. A colleague of hers suggested to her to get a live-in nanny. Unfortunately, when she broached the idea with Ray, he dismissed it as a very bad idea. This led to a shouting match in which the couple were yelling at each other only a few days earlier.

Desiree then felt that they could revisit the idea of the live-in nanny hoping they will not be having a contentious discussion as they drive to the wedding.

"Ray."

"Yes, what do you want?" Ray answered with a question in a sharp angry response. He was still trying to forget the time-wasting behavior of Desiree a few minutes earlier.

"Regarding the issue of us getting a live-in nanny…"

"So, what about it?" Ray interjected.

"What exactly is your problem?" Desiree blurted out. "You just can't handle the fact that I make money now and I don't need to wait on you for money anymore."

"Did you figure that out on your own? Or did the representatives from Single Mothers Network whispered it into your ears? When did you ever wait on me for money?

You have always had access to all bank accounts and all credit cards. So, what exactly is going on in your head?" Ray asked questions without waiting for answers.

"I am not asking you to pay the nanny. I will pay her salary myself," Desiree shouted at Ray.

"Obviously, you really don't know what you are talking about," Ray commented.

"Let us face it! It is my work, my life, my children, and I am paying the domestic assistant. So, what is your problem?"

"Of course, yes. You are a rich woman now. You are swimming with the sharks and dining with the lions of the human race, right? Is that why you can't see beyond your nose that you are misplacing your priorities?"

"What made you think that my having a successful career is a misplacement of priorities? I worked very hard for my accomplishments," Desiree asserted.

"Your hardworking and non-misplacement of priorities were obviously on full display when Bryan got detention for what he wrote instead of paying attention in class," Ray countered rhetorically.

"What happened?"

"Nothing happened."

"C'mon Ray! What did he do?"

"I thought you were here, you were there and you were everywhere for your kids!"

"Okay!" Desiree submitted in a harsh tone shaking her head. "What did he do?"

At the stop light, Ray took out his phone and pulled up the photograph he had taken of what Bryan wrote and gave his phone to Desiree to read for herself.

Bryan had written: "History repeated itself using language arts when chemistry decided to fight biology. Physics felt it was a wrong analysis explaining that mathematics made a wrong assumption about how economically viable social studies is. Computer tried its best to prevent the fight, but they made him look as if he was speaking a foreign language."

"Sounds interesting," Desiree remarked musing.

"Yeah. That was what he wrote on his answer sheet during a class test!"

"Oh my!" Desiree remarked sounding remorseful.

"When he was asked by his teacher about it, he said that he was missing his mum!"

"Hmmm!" Desiree sighed.

"I wonder where his mum was then and where she is now?" Ray asked rhetorically.

"Why are you so selfish?" Desiree blurted out.

"Me? Selfish? You must really be out of your mind!"

"Yes. You are being selfish. I supported your career all these years. I stayed at home to raise your children…"

"Only to abandon them when they needed you the most, right?" Ray interjected.

"If anything, that just proves my point that we should get a live-in nanny. I am not going to give up my career. You should be supportive of my career too!"

At that very moment, there was a blinding flash of light followed by an eardrum bursting sound of a thunder. Ray applied the brakes and slowed the car down in a reflex action to the thunderclap.

"Desiree! You are just too blind to see. Too short sighted to see beyond your nose. Too parochial to get the whole picture. I have always supported you, but you just didn't see it. Unfortunately, when you even saw it, and it was very clear to you, you still refused to acknowledge it. Now that you are working and you now have plenty of money, did you not do enough self-reflection to realize your stress level only went up? What exactly was the additional benefit that your abandoning the house has brought us as a family?"

"I did not abandon the family!" Desiree yelled.

"You can say whatever you want. You have a separate bank account only in your name now, right? You can spend your money the way you want now, right? However, let me be crystal clear to you. Whatever you felt you gained has only manifested itself to the rest of us as an absent wife to me and an absent mother to your children. Unfortunately, when you are even around for those few hours, you are cranky and impatient. You are now a heinous stressed out ghost that all we want to run away from."

"You are just exaggerating everything, and you are being unnecessarily dramatic," Desiree responded in an accusatory manner.

"I hope ....." Ray stopped his statement suddenly because a rider on a motorcycle wearing white gloves on his hands stopped the traffic in the direction Ray and Desiree were driving signaling for them to wait even when the light turns to green because of a funeral procession that has started passing through at that time.

Ray looked at Desiree and remarked, "I will give you a thousand dollars if you can show me that this funeral procession included a U-Haul vehicle moving the properties of the deceased to the grave to be buried along with the remains of the person."

Desiree simply turned her gaze away and looked out of the window on the passenger's side of the vehicle. She did not respond.

After the funeral procession ended, the light was still green in their direction of travel, so Ray crossed the intersection after the motorcycle rider who stopped them left.

He continued to address Desiree, "well, since you only listen to yourself and you only hear yourself as if you live permanently in an echo chamber, go ahead. I am very serious. Go ahead! Satisfy yourself. Feel free to go and hire your live-in nanny. I don't care who you hire whether she is Lassie, Cassie, Tassie or Jessie."

The rain stopped suddenly and then there was a loud noise.

Part Three: Section Three:
Who is at fault?

"All rise! The court is now in session. Judge Ayana Goodluck presiding," the court attendant announced.

Everybody in the court stood up momentarily.

"You may be seated," Judge Goodluck stated.

After a brief introduction of the court processes, the cases started.

Although this was a familiar territory for Ray after all he is a successful lawyer, but this was different and incredibly unexpected. He never foresaw that he would ever be in court as a defendant. However, here he was. He has being sued by his wife for a divorce. It was still a nightmare that he wished he could wake up from. Hard to believe that Desiree was asking to end her marriage to him after all he had been through with her and all he had done for her.

Desiree sat on the opposite side of the room wearing a red shirt underneath a Dolce & Gabbana black suit with pant. Her ebony black, highly shinning, Louboutin Lady Gena Red Sole Pumps completed her corporate look of success. However, her face was sullen. This was no happy event. Nonetheless, it was a task that must be completed no matter how unpleasant it may be. This has to end now. Negotiations are over. No doubt, irreparable damage has already occurred to her marriage of eighteen years. The divorce was inevitable. Desiree shook her head recognizing that her marriage actually died many years ago. The putrid corpse of the marriage was what has just been discovered and needed to be buried once and for all so that concerned parties can move on with their lives.

Ray threw a surreptitious glance at Desiree. She still looks as beautiful as ever, but the feeling was gone from his heart. He was not interested in her. He wished their case will be called quickly so that they can all leave, and he can put his nonsensical nightmare behind him.

Desiree also looked at Ray. She remembered when she bought him the light blue shirt that he wore to court and the striped alternating light blue and navy blue colored long necktie he was wearing. The navy-blue suit that he was wearing must have been new because Desiree had never seen it before that day.

Suddenly, her gaze met that of Ray. They looked at each other. Ray shook his head in displeasure and broke his gaze. Desiree was equally determined as she sat quietly beside her lawyer.

Ray could still not believe that he was in court to end the marriage that he had sacrificed so much for. He had given it everything he had. Maybe it was not meant to last till death or beyond it. Nonetheless it was too painful. This was certainly the endpoint that Kamal and Adam were hoping could be avoided. His buddies were not in court because he had chosen not to inform them. He knew this was an emotional gut punch that he had to take by himself. He was convinced that nothing could have saved his marriage so long as Desiree continued to be belligerent. He opined that he had gone above and beyond his duty as a husband for her. Ray recalled when Kamal suggested that he should buy hot lingerie for Desiree to turn her on for a chance for them to steer their marriage back on course to bliss.

"I have been there, done that. It did not work," Ray waived off the idea.

"But marriage experts tell us that women like it when their husbands buy them lingerie," Kamal defended his suggestion.

"It seems you did not pay attention. I just told you that I

have been through that road before. It was a dead end with Desiree."

"What happened?" Kamal inquired.

"Let's skip it," Ray tried to avoid the conversation.

"C'mon man!" Adam exclaimed. "Let us know what happened."

"Let us just say it is not as easy as it is made out to be and it is definitely not as effective as advertised. It was probably a gimmick brought about by lingerie manufacturers and distributors who are trying to get unsuspecting men to buy their products," Ray continued his rantings.

"C'mon Ray!" Adam persisted.

"Alright," Ray finally gave in. "I believe I went on that path not long after Bryan was born, and Desiree seemed to have forgotten that I existed in her world. The only thing that mattered to her were her three children. I had gone to meet an important client in Washington DC that gloomy day. I was in the waiting area and was feeling bored. I decided to browse a magazine on the center table. An article caught my attention. The author recommended buying lingerie for one's wife to rekindle the love flame. I really thought it was a great idea and decided to give it a shot. I went directly to *Euphoria Secret*.

"*Euphoria Secret* that was always being advertised on the television and magazines?" Adam sought confirmation.

"Yes. The same one with the catchy phrase: *Euphoria Secret*...ES is for the Extra Special lady in your life."

"Nice!" Adam exclaimed.

Ray simply shook his head and continued. "I went to the store in Arlington Shopping Center in Arlington. I was so excited, but on getting to the shop. I realized that I was ill-prepared."

"Why? What happened?" Kamal inquired.

"When I entered the store, there were so many displays of very attractive women modeling the lingerie. I mean...the models in the pictures were wearing only those bras and underwear. I really felt out of place..."

"Guilty pleasure?" Adam asked with tongue in cheek.

Ray simply ignored him and continued. "The all-female

attendants were very friendly and quite beautiful. Two young ladies came to me by the entrance to the store to ask how they may assist me. I told them that I wanted some lingerie…er ..er….well….hot and awesome for my wife."

Adam and Kamal chuckled.

"One of the ladies led me into the store and asked if I was looking for bras, underwear or nightclothes. I told her that I wanted all three. Then the bombshell."

"What?" Adam asked with surprise.

"She asked me her size."

"Okay?" Adam urged him on.

"That was when it hit me that…I actually did not know her size."

Kamal and Adam busted into laughter.

"Oh! It got worse than that," Ray continued. "By way of reflex action, I cupped my hands as if I could estimate her size and the three lady attendants near me started chuckling. It became clear immediately to me that I could not estimate her size. I was really embarrassed. Fortunately, these ladies were really on top of their games. They must have seen this 'show of shame' often enough. They calmed me down with their smiles and actually praised me for my effort which kinda made me feel better."

"Interesting!" Adam remarked.

"My attendant then suggested that I go home and look at her bra and panties to see her size since it would not be advisable to call Desiree and ask her for her size since that would ruin the surprise. I went home. Fortunately, I got home in the interval when Desiree had gone to pick the children from school. Rather than writing down a measurement which can be wrong, I just took a bra and a pantie from her lingerie chest and brought them to the *Euphoria Secret* store with me."

"Wow!" Adam exclaimed again.

"At this point for me, embarrassment was out of the way. I wanted to salvage the mission at all cost. So, using the sizes of the lingerie I brought, we chose six different provocative, elegantly designed 'wonder-bras', six 'eye-popping' panties and three 'see-through' sleepwear for Desiree."

"Awesome!" Adam exclaimed again unable to control his excitement.

"Well, I decided to make it a trifecta perfecta. I got her a *Ferrero Rocher* chocolate and completed the knockout with a blank card with a beautiful cover design. I poured my heartfelt loneliness-driven emotions in the card.

<u>My wish and my hope</u>

I wish
You see me
The way I see you
That does not mean you're blind

I wish
You feel for me
The way I feel about you
That does not mean you're insensitive

I wish
You think of me
The way I think of you
That does not mean you're dismissive

I wish
You hear me
The way I listen to you
That does not mean you're deaf

I wish
You love me
And reciprocate one percent of my love for you
That does not mean you have a heart of stone

I just don't know
How to make you know
How much I miss you
How much I love you

I hope you understand

Why I cannot withstand
You being away from me
And me being away from you.

It is because I love you.

"Outstanding!" Adam remarked. "How did she react?"

"It was horrible. Desiree was totally unappreciative. She remarked, 'does this look like what a woman will wear when breast feeding? Are trying to tell me that I am too fat, and you want me to lose weight quickly after childbirth. Is that why you bought me an underwear that I can't wear?'

"Apparently, the underwear that I took to the store were the ones she was wearing before she gave birth to Paige, our second child. She no longer wears them having gained some 'baby-induced' weights which she did not lose before giving birth to Bryan. Well, it turned out that she did not throw them away. Maybe she was hoping that one day, she would be able to wear them again or something like that. Unfortunately, they were the ones I took to *Euphoria Secret*. So, she was upset with me trying to insinuate that I was calling her fat and wanting to tell her to lose weight to be able to fit into what I bought her. Let us just say….it was a disaster! She did not want anything from me. I was too upset and too embarrassed to return them back to *Euphoria Secret*. I don't even know if you can return underwear anyway. I tried to explain how the whole thing happened, but she did not listen. I became angry too. So, I yelled at her and told her to return the items herself or give it away if she wanted. She only wore the sleepwear.

"How will she give underwear away to another lady?" Adam inquired.

"I didn't care. I was angry. I just yelled at her and slammed the door," Ray concluded.

Ray looked over again to where Desiree was sitting in the court and shook his head. He really gave this woman everything he had. Unfortunately, it was not good enough.

"The next case is Wright versus Wright," the court announcer proclaimed interrupting Ray's thought.

'Wright versus Wright' was about dissolution of a six-year marriage between William Wright and Wanda Wright. The back and forth conversations between the couple at times was funny even though they were discussing serious marital problems. The arguments and counterarguments were contentious. In the end, the request of the man was what made listeners laugh out loudly in the court. Surprisingly, even the presiding judge and the court reporter laughed too.

When Mr. William Wright was asked if he had anything else to say before the gavel came down. He replied that "I am happy that there is no child born as a product of this horrible marriage. No right-thinking person should bring a child into a marriage like this. It won't be right. Your honor, Wanda can keep everything she wants. However, I feel that it is my right to have the couch. I bought it on layaway, and it took me six months of hard labor to pay it off and own it outright. Also, I had slept on it a lot during the last five years of hell that this woman put me through. It is not memorabilia for me, it is my life, my comfort, my abode and my right."

Ray shook his head at the comment of the man. It seemed everything was "W" for "Wrong" with that marriage right from the very start. The couples were busy claiming their rights and not focusing on their responsibilities at all.

"Everybody has something to lose and something they want so bad. While rich couples fight over yachts and houses, poor couples fight over their couches. What a tale of two people!" Ray mused to himself.

Ray remembered his first time at the Organization for Oppressed Husbands (OOH) meeting in Annapolis. After he was welcomed into the infamous group of oppressed husbands, Mr Buster Ball asked him regarding his situation.

"I met my wife in college, and I love her so much. We married about thirteen years ago, but she seems to have lost interest in being married to me. However, it does not seem to me that she wants a divorce."

"You mean she wants to eat her cake and have it at the same time," Buster analyzed.

"Well, that seems very accurate. She will always deny me

her companionship...you know...I mean...almost everytime....
she is always saying '*No, leave me alone!*' She will insult me
whenever I insisted. A lot of time, she will deliberately make
the experience terrible in order to discourage me. Sometimes,
she will just lay down like a mannequin. The most irritating
scenario is typically when she did not really participate....
you know...when she is queen mannequin...I mean.... when
it is over.... she will then remark, 'is that all?'

"Wow!" Buster exclaimed.

"Yeah. She does that a lot..... just to annoy me."

"Brother, you are not alone. A lot of the guys you see
here have experienced similar abuses from their wives.
Unfortunately, the road is sometimes a dead end," Buster
painted a gloomy outlook.

"I am hoping that she will come to her senses that her
denying me her comfort duties is chipping away at the
foundation of our marriage," Ray expressed.

"I am guessing that you have tried the cards, the
chocolate and the lingerie routine," Buster asserted.

"Yes. They did not work," Ray regretted.

"Of course, they don't work," Buster confirmed.

"But why? Experts always tout them that they turn the
ladies on and make them come back to their husbands," Ray
queried.

"Those experts have no idea about what they are talking about.
I am not trying to be pessimistic, but only the woman can change
her mind about how she wants her marriage to be. There will be no
favorable end in sight if her mentality is that she is doing her
husband a favor or that she is being generous to him when she is
doing her comfort duties to him. It is ridiculous, but some women
really do believe that their husbands are lucky when they agree to
dance with them in between the sheets to the silent drums."

Ray was astonished and sought clarification. "Are you
saying that women ruin their marriages deliberately?"

"Maybe not deliberately, but the outcome is the same
anyway," Eduardo chimed in before Buster could respond.
Eduardo has been attending the OOH meeting for a while.
"You know that it is possible to be sincerely committed to an
error," Eduardo explained.

"Hmmm!" Ray sighed. "So, from your experience, how quickly do women get tired of their husbands?"

"Immediately after they have a child," Eduardo responded. "It sometimes feels as if that is their only objective of getting married. I will not be surprised at all to see that when human cloning becomes widespread, women will not even want any man near them again since they no longer have to go through that process they need us for anymore."

"Wow!" Ray exclaimed.

"Women tend to copy one another in error a lot. Sometimes, they are unsuspecting that the person advising them may not have their best interest at heart at all. Sometimes, it is just that they hide their true nature from their husbands until such a time that they feel empowered to reveal who they really are," Eduardo explained further.

"The sad and totally pathetic part is that women abuse their husbands with their '*No! Leave me alone!*' and then they feign ignorance so that they can claim to be shocked that their husbands are thinking of other women," Buster commented.

"Every man thinks about other women. They just don't talk about it and most men will not pursue it," Eduardo asserted.

"Of course, that is true," Buster agreed. "If a man is asked by his wife if he thinks about other women, his best move is not to respond at all or change the topic of the conversation. Not many men can come up with an ingenious answer on the fly."

"Oh! Why?" Ray inquired.

"Because if he says '*yes*', he is stupid and if he says '*no*', he is a liar," Buster explained.

"However, these women who constantly pelt their husbands with the infamous '*No! Leave me alone!*' abuses often help their husbands get over the hurdle of translating thoughts about other women into action. By the time they come to their senses and realized that there are many women out there who wouldn't say '*no*', it may be too late because the beast might have left the cardboard cage called *pristine monogamy* for *free-range monogamy*!" Eduardo commented with slight anger in his voice.

Ray was wondering what an ingenious answer would be for the question when his thought was interrupted.

"The next case is Desiree Marshall versus Ray Marshall!" the court announcer proclaimed.

Ray came to his senses in the present when his case was called. He and his lawyer got up and moved forward. Desiree and her lawyer stood up and moved forward too.

Ray sighed. He genuinely felt that had done everything a husband could do for his wife. Albeit he was an imperfect man, he had given the relationship everything he had. Unfortunately, they had grown apart and the center can no longer hold. They need to go their separate ways to different happy homes.

Desiree's premise for divorce centered around her claim of infidelity by Ray. She accused him of having an affair with Jessie, the live-in nanny she hired. In a sworn affidavit, Desiree had claimed that she had long suspected that an extramarital affair was going on between Ray and her former live-in nanny. She stated that she was at home one day when Ray said, 'Sweetie.' To her surprise, both her and Jessie replied, 'yes' in unison. It made her wonder what must have been going on in her absence.

"Your honor!" Desiree continued, "I overheard a phone conversation between Jessie and one of her girlfriends. 'Do people lose their brain with more education?' Jessie had asked her friend. 'I thought they were supposed to be smarter. Look at the lady of this house, she kept leaving her home to me. I do everything around here from cooking to the entire home management. I do the laundry including her husband's underwear. I even lay her husband's bed. Well, I might as well sleep in it too. I am doing everything else for him anyway.' It made me more suspicious."

Desiree recalled that she confronted her husband and asked him point blank, "are you having an affair with the maid?"

"I didn't know that we have a maid," Ray replied.

"I am talking about *Jessie the Jezebel*," Desiree responded with a profound anger in her voice.

"I thought you call her a *Domestic Assistant*. So, when did she become a maid?"

"Just answer the question!"

"You must be out of your mind to ask me such an insulting, nonsensical, accusatory question!"

"Are you having an affair with the maid?" Desiree repeated her question.

"I will not dignify that stupid question with a response," Ray responded as he walked away.

"Your honor, he did not deny the allegation," Desiree asserted and continued her narration. "One day I came home unannounced and my husband and Jessie were dancing to Mambo Jambo Number Eight, that stupid song which depicts the mindset of stupid men."

This is Mambo Jambo number 8

One, two, three, four
Wow! Wow! Wow! Wow!
I am not going away
I am here to stay
My dear, make my day

Hit it!

A tiny piece of Desiree is good enough
A tiny piece of Jessie is good for me
A tiny piece of Ariana is what I want
A tiny piece of Jenifer all day long
A tiny piece of Aliyah everyday

Five, six, seven, eight
Wow! Wow! Wow! Wow!
I am not going away
I am here to stay
My dear, make my day

Hit it!

A tiny piece of Brianna in my house
A tiny piece of Aneesa in my shed
A tiny piece of Olivia in my cave
A tiny piece of Alfreda rocks my world
A tiny piece of you makes me a happy man

One, two
I want you too
Three, four
I want some more

Five, six
Love is a fix
Seven, eight
Loving you is my fate.

Hit it!
Wow! Wow! Wow! Wow!
I am not going away
I am here to stay
My dear, make my day

It was surprising to the judge that Ray had not put up much defense during all the deliberations. He constantly said that what he wanted was the same thing that Desiree wanted. He emphasized that it would be better for them to part ways and both of them can go and find their happiness elsewhere. The only time he spoke as a form of defense, he merely gave Desiree's schedule to the judge.

"Your honor! My wife is only available as a wife and mother of five children from 10 PM to 5 AM on weekdays and from 10 PM to 8 AM on the weekends."

"What did you mean?" The judge sought clarification.

"Well your honor! Kindly let me share my wife's work schedule with you and let everybody reflect whether her self-adopted work-life balance is compatible with being a happily married woman with growing children. My wife will work from Monday to Friday as the Marketing Manager for *MMM Holdings Inc.* leaving home at 6 AM and returning home after 8 PM in the evening. On Saturdays and Sundays, she worked tirelessly on establishing her start-up company. Now, she has established *Cosmos Cosmetics* and she partners with a distributor in King Business Plaza in Mount Vernon selling cosmetics from 9 AM to 9 PM on weekends."

"That does not give you the right to be messing around with the live-in nanny," Desiree's legal counsel argued.

"That is what you chose to believe," Ray replied. "What I need is a wife, not an accountant, a business executive or a billionaire. She can keep her money, her education and whatever she thinks she has. All I ever wanted was for her to be a loving wife and a wonderful mother to our children. Since being a wife or a good mother is no longer her priority, she is free to leave. All I want is to be free to move on too."

"Why did you wait for so long in this marriage then?" the Judge asked Ray.

"I foolishly believed in a concept that I read from somewhere a long time ago that, 'if you are not prepared to take the hurt that comes with being in love, then you are not ready to taste the sweetness that comes from it either.' I know better now that arrogant people don't change until their circumstances change. Indeed, pride goes before a fall."

All the deliberations and the negotiations have now concluded. The presiding judge was making her statements regarding their divorce and was about to rule on their case when something struck Desiree. Somehow, it suddenly struck her that she made a big mistake. She looked at Susan who had come to court to support her in her divorce proceedings. Susan simply shrug her shoulders. Although Ray will be paying child support for his children, the court was going to ask her to contribute to the family expenses since she makes decent money too whereas Ray was the one paying all the family bills previously. That simply means that Ray will now be spending less money than what he used to spend on his family. No alimony was awarded because she makes a good income too. Furthermore, while she is happy that her children will be staying with her, Ray has visitation rights. However, the worst part of the divorce is that Ray will now simply be free to marry Jessie who is a twenty-two-year old lady as her replacement in his life. Afterall, she is already familiar with him. Jessie is eighteen years younger than her and she is in her hot prime. Now, all her actions did not make much sense anymore. Maybe that was why Ray was not really struggling to stop her from divorcing him, she surmised.

Bang! The judge slams the gavel concluding her ruling.

It was as if the sound shocked Desiree into the reality that has just unfolded. The sound snapped Desiree out of her trance. Desiree started sweating boulders and she busted into tears.

"No. Please no! I don't want a divorce anymore. Ray, I am sorry. I am so sorry," Desiree mustered. As if in a flash, Desiree remembered when Ray made her read a poem that he had written for her at a *Feed the Homeless* event in college. He had pretended that he had written it for someone else, so that she could read the poem without reading any meaning into it. She also remembered what he did when she did not give him an immediate response after his marriage proposal. She had told him that she will think about it and that she still had some lingering questions. The following day, he had wooed her by asking 'her questions' on her behalf and answering them himself without any input from her.

Questions with answers
Is my falling in love with you a message?
Yes. From my heart to your heart for marriage
Are we destined to be together?
Yes. For we are better together

What will our lives be with each other?
Wonderful! We belong with each other
How will things be for us as a couple?
Perfect! We will not have any trouble

How many children should we have?
Twelve children and they won't starve
What will my life be without you?
I don't want to find out, neither should you.

As people started making their way out of the courtroom, Desiree's yelled again. "Ray! I am so sorry. I don't want to find out too!"

Ray looked at her with profound sadness on his face. He shook his head as a wave of goodbye. He turned his back and started walking towards the door to exit out of the courtroom too.

Desiree started walking briskly across the court towards him shouting on top of her lungs. "I was confused. I did not know what I was doing. I listened to bad advice. It was my fault all along. I did not do my duties to him. Judge, please I withdraw my petition. I am very sorry."

As she ran towards Ray, the police officer in charge of court proceedings security stopped her.

"Mam, not here! You have to go and find another avenue to talk to him."

Desiree continued crying. "I am sorry Ray." She shouted even more. There was an uproar of some sort in the court room at the strange turn of events. Many of the people in the court were dumbfounded. They had never witnessed anything bizarre like that before, but Desiree was undeterred. "Ray! Ray!!" she continued to shout trying to get his attention. Ray continued to walk away with his attorney without looking back.

Like in a flash, Desiree remembered the last card Ray gave her the day before she insisted that he must pack his stuff out of their marital home. She had told him that they had reached the end of their marriage. He was frantically trying to salvage their marriage, but she was done.

Look, hold and behold
Don't go away
Let me look at you
Let me see the sunshine in your face

Don't slip away
Let me see you
Let me see the moonlight in your eyes

Don't move away
Let me gaze upon you
Let me see the sparkling stars in your teeth

Don't walk away
Let me observe you
Let me see the wind blowing from your hair

Don't shift away
Let me look at you
Let me see your pretty tiara

Don't run away
Let me hold and behold you
Let me see, feel and touch all your treasures

I love you

Now, she realized her blunder, but he seemed to have lost interest in her.

"I am sorry. I am sorry. I will be a better wife. Please don't leave. She wanted to keep going towards him, but the police officer held her right hand restraining her movement. She stretched out her left hand trying to grab Ray, but the grasp of the police officer was too strong. Desiree could not reach Ray who lowered his head and kept walking away without looking back. Desiree continued to sob with the officer still holding her right hand. She looked up and saw Susan leaving the courtroom with a flat affect. No pity on her face at all. No remorse. Desiree felt more heart broken. This was indeed a costly blunder and she had nobody to blame but herself. She did not get her priorities right.

"No! No! No! I don't want a divorce. Ray, come back!" Desiree continued to shout trying to free herself from the cop in order to follow Ray. There was a big commotion in the court as people started gathering around Desiree, thereby obstructing her view. The cop who was holding her hand started calling for back up response from other officers.

All of a sudden, her sight became clear and her view was good. It was as if she just opened her eyes with too much light entering her eyes. Desiree became confused. Ray was holding her right hand tightly and he then grabbed her left hand too while he was shouting for help of some sort. He was shouting for the nurses to come to his aid. Desiree continued to thrash around in the bed frantically trying to get up. Five nurses rushed into the room like swarming bees on stinging emergency response. One of them went out to get something. Ray continued to hold both her hands while saying things to her that she could not understand. She wondered what was going on. The heart monitor was alarming as if the whole world was on fire. The infusion pump appeared to be competing with the heart monitor in producing the most annoying sound that can drive the whole world insane. Everything was chaotic. Desiree was puzzled. She did not know whether to be happy seeing Ray holding her hands after he just walked out of the courtroom without looking back.

"Desiree calm down! I am here! You are not in a court. You are in the hospital. I am not divorcing you," Ray continued to repeat his statements. "You have been in a coma for about a week. There was an accident. You had head injury," Ray tried to bring Desiree up to speed to quickly catch up with what was going on. He tried summarizing a week-long event into a one-minute precis.

Desiree did not understand what was going on. She kept crying and sobbing. Begging Ray not to leave her. Saying that she can see clearly now. She will change for the better. Ray thought it was the effect of sudden emergence from coma, but he wondered why his wife was shouting about someone named *Jessie*. The nurse that left came back with a medication which she gave immediately through the intravenous line to calm Desiree down.

As the effect of the medication started kicking in, Desiree held on tight to Ray's hand and remarked, "please don't leave me. I am very sorry. We can work it out. Don't leave me for *Jessie*."

Ray replied with tear laden eyes, "I don't know who *Jessie* is. I am not going anywhere baby. I am right here with you. This is where I belong."

This brought a smile to Desiree's face as she gradually closed her eyes falling asleep from the effect of the medication the nurse gave her.

Ray was happy as he released Desiree's hands after he was certain that she had fallen asleep. The long road to recovery has just begun. At least, she has now awakened from coma. The next step will be to explain what happened to her.

Of wisdom and patience
Knowing not to go to a useless war
Is the peak of wisdom
For a strong Army General

Knowing to be content with little
Is the peak of wisdom
For a person who wants to be happy

Knowing to love one's family
Is the peak of wisdom
For the one who wants to be beloved

Knowing that after every hardship comes relief
Is the peak of wisdom
For the one who wants to survive

Knowing to be steadfast, patient, and prayerful
Is the peak of wisdom
For a couple going through challenges

Be wise, be patient.

Epilogue

"**O**uch!" Desiree shouted suddenly when the physical therapist touched a tender point in her right shoulder while giving her a massage.

"I am so sorry," the therapist apologized. She then reassured Desiree that her neck and shoulder will get better with time, but she should continue to perform the exercises that she had been teaching her.

Desiree could still not believe her ears while listening to what her husband was telling her regarding the accident that happened two weeks previously.

"We did not make it to the wedding, right?" Desiree asked again for the umpteenth time still trying to put the pieces together in her mind.

"Yes. We did not make it to the wedding. We were about three miles from the venue when the accident happened. We had been arguing about your decision to hire a live-in nanny since you had been so busy with work. You barely had any time for yourself, let alone your children and I definitely was no longer on your list of important people...."

"C'mon Ray!" Desiree interjected. "I am very sorry." Desiree then placed her left hand on Ray right hand to affirm her genuine apology.

"Well," Ray continued, we were crossing an intersection after a funeral procession when a spoiled brat driving a brand-new Chevy Camaro hit us. He just got the car as his eighteenth birthday gift and was acting his own version of 'fast and foolish' by attempting a 'no look drive to the intersection' while trying to impress his girlfriend. Unfortunately, he drove into us as we were crossing the intersection hitting the passenger side of our vehicle. That was when you lost consciousness from a head injury. You started saying all sorts of things that did not make sense a few hours before you actually woke up. In particular, you kept mentioning somebody whose name is *Jessie*."

"It was surreal. It felt so real," Desiree remarked with a sigh.

"Who is *Jessie*?" Ray asked Desiree.

"Nobody I want you to meet," Desiree replied.

After two weeks in the rehabilitation center, Desiree came

home. She was met with pomp and pageantry. The children decorated the house with many "Welcome Home Mummy" signs and they had many "Get Well Soon" balloons.

Desiree took some time off from work to recuperate. One day, she starred out of the window when it was raining. She watched with a new appreciation of life as the branches and the leaves of the Cherry tree danced to the wind of the heavy downpour. She was re-reading a card that Ray had given her about three years earlier. It was one of those "make -up" cards that she had received from Ray after a fight, an all too common occurrence in their marriage.

If only you know
If only you notice
If only you discern
If only you're informed about
If only you perceive
If only you recognize
If only you're conscious of
If only you see
If only you comprehend
If only you're familiar with
If only you sense
If only you register
If only you're acquainted with
If only you're aware
If only you realize
How beautiful you are when you smile
You will never frown at me

If only you know
How much I love you
You will never leave my side

I love you

Desiree's heart responded, "Ray, now I know. Now, I know. I am just glad that it was not too late." She folded the card and put it back into its envelope and closed the curtains.

"Life is short, and happiness comes from within!" Desiree remarked loudly shaking her head as tears rolled down her cheeks. "Is Susan a true friend or a jealous homewrecker?" she asked herself.

Author's note: Is Susan a true friend or a jealous homewrecker?

Adam and Aneida got out of the car and started walking towards the entrance of Riverdale Mall in Alexandria. Suddenly, the sight of a young lady pushing a baby stroller caught his attention.

"Excuse me for a minute!" Adam said to Aneida and he quickened his pace towards the lady.

"Hi Nora!" Adam greeted her with a broad smile.

"Hi Adam!" Nora replied with an element of surprise on her face.

"How are you?"

"I am fine. Thank you," she replied.

"How is everybody at home? Your mum? Your dad? Norma? Richard?" Adam asked questions in close succession without waiting for an answer out of excitement.

"Dad is doing fine, but I am not on speaking terms with mum at this time. We are staying in our corners."

"Huh!" Adam expressed surprise at the response he got from Nora.

Nora continued, "as per Richard, we are not together anymore." Nora paused for a few seconds, sighed, and then continued. "We were married for only 11 months. He walked away two months before his son was born. I understand that he lives in New York now."

Adam did not know what to say. These were not the answers he was expecting to hear. He definitely did not want to stir up a hornet's nest by probing for more information. So, he bent down towards the baby in order hide his surprise while trying to change the subject.

"So, how is life in general?" Adam mustered.

"So-so. We are surviving," Nora responded.

He played with the child by rubbing his belly gently making the baby giggle. The baby held on tightly to his right index finger. He then asked, "what is his name?"

"Adam," Nora replied with a broken voice.

Adam almost choked on his saliva when he heard Nora's response. He was taken completely by surprise. He tried to understand why the baby was given his name, but he could not ask that question because of the presence of Aneida who had now arrived where they were. Maybe, he really did not need to ask.

Adam got up from his squatting position and introduced Aneida to Nora.

"Nora, please meet Aneida, my wife. Aneida, this is Nora. She was Sarah's fourth grade teacher and arguably, her favorite and best teacher ever."

Waa! Waa! Waa! The annoying and loving cries of babies filled the air from their cribs. It appeared as if the twins were in competition to determine who can cry louder. Kamal rolled onto his left side and put a pillow over his head while Bonita got up to attend to the crying babies in their cribs.

"Didn't you just feed these babies?" Kamal asked as if he really needed an answer.

"Well, they are hungry again," Bonita responded.

"Should we sign them up for gastric bypass surgery so that they can stop eating so much and stop bothering us?"

"Sure! Great idea. Call your favorite psychiatrist first. I am sure you know that once you reduce their stomach capacity, then they will need to eat more frequently," Bonita replied poking fun at Kamal.

"Darn it! You are right. Hmmm!" Kamal sighed as he rolled over again.

"You wanted busloads of children, remember?" Bonita recalled as she picked Jack up after gently rocking Jacklyn in the crib. This was Bonita's way of reassuring Jacklyn that she had not been forgotten

186

Kamal had no answer. He just wanted the little babies to stop disturbing his sleep.

"Jack seemed to eat a lot more than Jacklyn already," Bonita continued as she started breastfeeding.

"I guess it is the Y-chromosome then," Kamal suggested.

Suddenly, Jacklyn started crying again.

"It would have been wonderful, if only you could breastfeed Jacklyn while I am breastfeeding Jack," Bonita regretted.

"Would you like me to try?" Kamal suggested with sarcasm.

"Yes, please."

Kamal went to the crib and picked Jacklyn up as if he was really going to breastfeed her. To his utmost surprise, Jacklyn stopped crying immediately after Kamal picked her up. Kamal was puzzled.

"You don't think Jacklyn heard us and she truly believed that I was going to breastfeed her, do you?" Kamal asked Bonita being quite surprised at the turn of events.

'C'mon Kamal! She wanted a loving cuddle from her dad as she awaits her turn at the nipple."

"Phew!" Kamal exhaled jokingly.

Suddenly, the atmosphere was interrupted by the melodious ringing tune of Kamal's phone which was on the table in the bedroom. The clock on Bonita's dresser revealed six forty-five in the morning. He wondered who could be calling him so early in the morning on a Saturday.

Kamal walked up to the table and picked the phone. He shook his head disappointingly on recognizing the caller.

"I don't think you want to see your son again!" Kandie blurted out. "You have not been returning my calls. You have not been coming to see him. I am going to tell my lawyer to petition for me to have sole custody again."

Kamal took the phone briefly away from his ears as he felt disturbed by Kandie's ranting. However, Kandie continued undeterred with an enormous anger in her voice.

"In fact, if you don't come and see him by tomorrow, I am going to change his name to Jamal," Kandie threatened.

At this Kamal simply hung up the phone.

Bonita could sense that the call was from Kandie, but she was very comfortable in her space. She knew that she did not need to dabble into whatever the issue was between Kamal and Kandie at all. Staying in her lane was the sensible thing for her to do.

Kandie threw her phone on the bed when she realized that Kamal had hung up on her. She looked at the phone with disgust. Then, she picked it up again and re-dialed Kamal repeatedly. However, all her calls simply went into Kamal's voicemail. Kandie became frustrated. She wondered why men do not feel for their children the way women feel for their children. It was as if men do not see their children, independent of their mothers. It seemed that the love children get from their father, to a great extent, is conditional on the love between their father and their mother. If it is not existing, it will be hard to have any love flowing from the father to his children.

Kamal felt that Kandie behaved like a stupid telemarketer who was selling a baby product that he could do without. He smiled at Bonita without saying a word about the phone call he just received. He gave Jacklyn to Bonita since Jack has suckled a bit so that Jacklyn can get some breast milk too.

Kamal looked at Bonita and smiled. He truly felt lucky and blessed with her. He thought of something which made him chuckle.

"What?" Bonita asked him, being puzzled.

"I was thinking of a statement that I have heard before, but I do not remember where I heard it from."

"What is the statement?" Bonita inquired being curious.

"Everything in the world is beautiful, but nothing in the world compares to a virtuous woman," Kamal related.

"I also don't know who said so, but I am in total agreement with him or her," Bonita expressed laughing.

"I actually think that it was a statement of a respectable and revered statesman. I just don't remember who said so," Kamal regretted.

"Such a beautiful statement coming from a man.... makes it... even more special," Bonita chuckled.

"I agree," Kamal submitted, but he continued to wonder who said the statement.

THE END OF BOOK 3

Afterword

Reflections of the author

Dear readers:

It has been a great journey in the last four years hanging with the three guys who were talking about their love lives. This was a fictional work that was set in our modern-day reality. The main motivation for this work was the realization that many marriages in the Western Hemisphere face enormous challenges because of the changing dynamics in our social milieu. However, some of the challenging issues we confront are not simple. There are important physiological differences between males and females that actually drive the way we see the world and how we interact with it. Unfortunately, it is very obvious that men often do not openly discuss issues that affect them in their marriages even during marital counseling sessions. Many men wait to the last minute to just act out their frustrations. Occasionally, things get addressed early enough to save these marriages, but more often than not, things would only come to light when irreparable damages have been done.

Indeed, I have heard a lot of questions, comments, and suggestions from readers over the years regarding the first two books. I have listened to lots of personal reflections of readers at book signings and other public and private gatherings. I must say that different aspects of this work touched many peoples' lives beyond my imagination. To all my readers, I say a heartfelt thank you. To my lady consultants and those who shared their life stories with me, I am greatly indebted to you. To those who gave me feedback and suggestions, I truly appreciate your help and support.

My original intention was simply to write a short-lived love story between Adam and Nora that lasted for only one week, but written from the viewpoint of Adam. I actually wrote over a hundred poems and love notes from Adam to Nora before I started writing the manuscript for this trilogy. The pristine love that Adam had for Nora was the original story that eventually got expanded to three guys talking about their relationships. From talking with readers (men and women alike), most people expressed that the story of Ray and Desiree resonated with them the most.

I decided to look at these everyday relationship issues unapologetically from men's point of view. This is because, typically, men have challenges in showing emotions especially when it is related directly to them. Unfortunately, this can be problematic for relationships when difficulties arise. Hence, in this literary work, I decided to present mens' viewpoints on many common everyday relationship scenarios in our modern lives. It is my sincere hope that I accomplished same without offending anybody's sensibility. However, I hope that I was able to convey the core general messages of this trilogy:

Number one: It may not take too much to please your man.
Number two: Men are highly unlikely to give up a lovely wife for anything.
Number three: Love is an indescribable feeling that has no boundaries.

Regarding the trilogy, the stories of the three guys were written from passion, emotion, and imagination. Book one, "my wife or my children's mother?" was about highlighting love and emotional challenges that men often have, but generally don't want to talk about. Book two, "when ladies fight back" was about how men try to adjust and adapt to their situations with ideas that sometimes don't work the way they expect. It also gave insight into what women can do to avoid losing their husbands by highlighting the weakness of men. A core message was demonstrated by Bonita. It is foolhardy to fight your husband when he is having any challenge with another lady outside the home except you just wanted to end your own relationship. This is because you would have just ruined his place of solace with such a fight. Your best bet is to figure a way for him to be with you and not away from you. Finally, book three, 'the romantic tragedy' was about dealing with consequences which men often see coming but they are too powerless to avoid.

On a jocular note, the most common question I often get was about which of the three guys represented me (smile). The truth is that none of the three guys represented anybody that I know or have heard of in any way, shape, or form. However, I do understand that although the characters in the trilogy are fictional, the issues presented are painful realities that some people have experienced or are still experiencing. I personally hope and pray that those having these relationship challenges get the succor they surely desire.

Regarding the "Author's notes" in the novels, they were meant to be reflection and discussion points especially between couples after reading the novel. Most of these questions have no set answers. Each couple need to chart their own path to their desired successful marriage.

However, as a bonus feature, I am going to answer only one of these authors' notes.

> **Author's Note:** If a husband and wife are eating together, what percentage of the food is generally consumed by the husband and what percentage of the food is consumed by the wife?
>
> **My answer:** The husband eats 100% of the food when he is hungry, and the wife eats 0% of the food when she is in love (smile).

Finally, I want to give a loud shout out to my wonderful daughter. I often affectionately refer to her as my personal bodyguard. She was always inspirational to me and made many suggestions to me in the course of writing this trilogy including the pictures too. We took some of the actual journeys referenced in this trilogy together. In particular, our father-daughter one week get away road trip to many destinations all the way to the Niagara Falls was truly an adventure to treasure forever. In case you are wondering, ...yes, she does not like to wash plates (smiles).

From the top and bottom of my heart, from each of my ventricles, I say a truly heartfelt, "Thank you all."

With love,
Adeyinka O. Laiyemo, MD, MPH

ABOUT THE AUTHOR

Dr. Adeyinka O. Laiyemo is an Associate Professor of Medicine. He is a gastroenterologist and practices medicine in the District of Columbia. However, his heart is in art. He was a writer for The Daily Champion in Nigeria in the nineties. His poems have been published in anthologies in the United States.

Adeyinka loves comedy, poetry, and enjoys traveling.

Three Guys Talking Trilogy

Novels in the series